LASSITER: RIMFIRE

Want to commit suicide? The quickest way is to tangle with Lassiter. He wasn't born mean, but he learned easily. He's no meaner than the times he lives in, no dirtier than the men he's killed. Not that Lassiter frets about dead men, because he's never killed a man who didn't need killing — more or less. He's everything you would expect a hero not to be — he's a new breed of Westerner.

JACK SLADE

LASSITER: RIMFIRE

Complete and Unabridged

LINFORD
Leicester

First published in the
United States of America

First Linford Edition
published November 1992

Copyright © 1968 by Belmont Productions, Inc.

British Library CIP Data

Slade, Jack
    Lassiter: Rimfire.—Large print ed.—
Linford western library
I. Title II. Series
813.54 [F]

ISBN 0–7089–7259–4

Published by
F. A. Thorpe (Publishing) Ltd.
Anstey, Leicestershire
Set by Words & Graphics Ltd.
Anstey, Leicestershire
Printed and bound in Great Britain by
T. J. Press (Padstow) Ltd., Padstow, Cornwall

1

THEY watched him come off the dry lake, seeing him first as a black fly speck moving alone on the white alkali. They watched because there was nothing else to look at, but they didn't believe. It was mid-afternoon and the heat waves rolling up from the level packed floor made vision and the judging of distance unreliable. Heat drugged the town that wormed along the tracks between the lake and the towering row of mountains hedging in its rear.

They sat on their heels, their backs against the buckling walls of the raw wood buildings, sat like waiting buzzards hopeful that some carcass would fall at their feet.

They sat because it was Saturday and any rider must come to town on Saturday. They sat because they had already expended their small money stock and there was nothing else to do in Puente.

Puente had four excuses for existing where it did. The railroad engineers had found the lake and welcomed the long, flat shoreline, had veered their grade down the eastern mountains and run their line for thirty miles on the level before they had to take it up again through the pass in the western wall. They had built their division point here. There were springs here, fed by the underground river that followed down the mountain's bedrock and lost itself in the insatiable sand. There were mines back in the hills and fertile valleys made green by small rushing streams, sheltering ranches where cattle fed.

The railroad, the springs, the mines, the ranches fathered the bastard town. One single building deep, three blocks long, the shacks that grew up around the railroad yard huddled along the curving rails, facing across them towards the endless, arid lake. Someone had called the collection Puente. No one remembered why, nor cared. There was no ghost or civic pride. Not one of the people who used the place as home would not move out at the whisper of a chance.

Lassiter walked into the town from the dry lake. Seventy miles he had walked. In the wrong direction. He was glad to be there. He stepped across the tracks, crossed the road and came up onto the wood sidewalk. He turned and followed it. He passed in front of the row of watching men without appearing to notice them. He walked a straight course in the shambling straightness of a tireless bear. The boots were worn out. They had a right to be. He had walked them for eighteen hours. They were not his, nor were the shapeless clothes that looked as if they belonged to a shorter, heavier man. They had.

He did not know the name of the town. He did not care. He was glad it was there. He had crossed the lake that the sheriff had said nobody could cross on foot. He had walked it, in a country where a man seldom traveled a hundred yards without climbing on his horse. He was alive. He meant to stay alive.

The men he passed watched with grave interest, trying to read the sign. They were curious, but in this land no one asked. He walked, and this they did not understand. He looked as if he had walked far. He had come off the lake, but where had he entered it? They thought he must have dropped off a passing freight somewhere outside of town, but no freight had passed that afternoon, and they had first seen him a mile out on the scorching lake. The thermometer on the hotel wall said a hundred and twenty-eight.

They studied his dusty, ill fitting clothes, his blistered face half concealed in the black whiskers four days old, his broken hat, his broken boots, his lack of gear, lack of canteen. Their minds would not even suggest that he had walked from Harmony, seventy-two miles straight across the lake.

Mostly they stared at his waist. He wore no gun belt. He had no gun. No man except a bum traveled this country without a gun.

Lassiter reached the hotel. He did not turn in at the narrow, dark lobby, into the superheated, trapped air. He went on to the passage, littered with blown tumble-weed, papers, cans, filth, that ran beside the building and dead-ended in the sharp mountainside just behind it.

A wash bench sat against the rear wall, a granite basin and three buckets filled with water. Lassiter stopped before the nearest bucket. He raised it and drank. He drank from the brim, slow, in measured swallows. Held the water in his mouth, let it trickle back. His throat was too parched for the muscles to have control. He allowed himself three drinks. His body begged in spasms for more.

He put the bucket on the bench,

bent and buried his head in it. The water was tepid, stale, sulphurous. But it was wet. It stung the blistered skin under his mat of beard. He held his face in it until he had to breathe. He came up, water coming with him. It coursed down into his neck, across the sorry clothes. He savored that. He plunged hands and forearms into the pail. Displaced water slopped over the rim. He held out his boot to catch it, tipped the pail to spill into the other boot.

His hands were large, big knuckled, with long, square tipped fingers, strong. He flexed them in the water, letting the cured skin soak up as much as it would hold. He withdrew his hands and lifted the bucket to his mouth again.

He was being observed by a woman from an upper hotel window. He did not care. Again he ducked his head and this time scrubbed some of the alkali from his beard and hair. Finally he straightened. He had not had enough water. His body told him it would never again have enough water. He knew he dared not drink more now.

He poured water down the back of his shirt. He stretched the waist of his pants and emptied the bucket down the inside of his legs. He turned back to the street, feeling the damp clothes act like an olla, the evaporation cooling his body somewhat. Such was the heat that before he reached the saloon door his clothes were dry.

The squatting men watched as he passed again. When he turned into the saloon they were surprised. Some rose to follow.

The room was shadowed. That was the best to be said for it. It stank of human sweat, damp sawdust, spilled beer that gave back the smell of urine. Tobacco smoke added to the hot air made it difficult to breathe. Yet there were a dozen men at the scarred bar.

Lassiter stopped just inside the batwing door. He knew that the men from the street were behind. He did not turn. He knew what was in their minds. They were bored with the heat, with inaction. They were looking for trouble.

The room was noisy with forced laughter, men trying to prove to themselves that they were having a good time. They weren't.

Lassiter advanced to the bar. Boots behind him shuffled through the sawdust. A man came against the counter on either side of him. Both were bigger than he was. He stood only five feet eleven.

The man on his right said, "Stranger, ain't you?"

Lassiter looked at him.

"Saw you come off the lake. Lose you horse?"

"I walked."

The man's eyes darkened. "Across that lake? Walked? Nobody ever did that."

"I did." Lassiter turned away.

"I don't like a liar. Do you like a liar, Abner?" The man's voice was up. It carried down the crowd. It stopped the laughter. The men waited. Lassiter knew what they waited for. A fight. The free entertainment of a fight.

He was too tired for anger. He turned very slowly. He reached out, almost a friendly gesture. The fingers of his right hand touched the man's forearm just below the elbow. The man looked uncertain. Lassiter's left hand shot out and caught the wrist. The man jerked back, but both Lassiter's hands bit into the arm. With a sudden movement he raised the arm and brought it down against the edge of the bar. Hard.

The bone snapped. It sounded like a dry stick snapping. The sound crossed the room before the sharp yelp of pain drowned it.

Lassiter threw the man into the two men standing behind him. He turned back to the startled bartender.

"Set them up. For the house. Whiskey for me."

A concerted stalking had begun, closing in. It stopped. How could you take a man who was buying you a drink? The room was quiet. Down the bar they stood looking at him. An unexpected host. Even the man with the broken arm straightened and stared.

As the drinks were poured some raised their glasses in silent salute. Lassiter acknowledged them only by lifting his glass and draining it, motioning for a refill.

"Do it again."

The bartender hurried. Nothing like this had happened in Puente in a long time.

Lassiter finished his drink while the bartender was still busy pouring others. He put down the glass and moved towards the door. The man with the broken arm watched him, silent. Lassiter was shoving the door apart when the bartender saw him.

"Hey . . . "

Lassiter pointed a finger at the man farthest along the bar. "He's buying."

The bartender looked at the man.

The man straightened. "Hell," he

10

said out of surprise. "I never saw him before."

The bartender scooped up the bung starter. "Let's get him." He started for the door. No one else moved.

The bartender erupted into the sun-charged street in his dirty apron. He expected Lassiter to be running. He wasn't. He stood in the shade of the wooden awning, looking at nothing.

The bartender stopped. You didn't just rush up and hit a man with a bung starter if he was just standing there, not looking at you. Not if you remembered the broken arm. He went forward warily.

"Why the hell did you do that to me?"

"I needed a drink."

"You didn't have to set up for the whole town." Anger made the bartender's voice thick.

"Would you have given me a drink if I'd asked?"

"No, but . . . "

"But you slopped it out fast enough

when you thought I'd pay for the house. And I had to stop that fight."

"What fight?"

"The one that would have started in the next second. Think about it. Your spot would have been wrecked."

Lassiter turned his back and walked toward the yellow railroad station. The bartender opened his mouth to yell. Then he stopped. There would have been a fight, that was so. The saloon would have been wrecked. It had been wrecked before. He swore and went back inside. No one paid attention to him. They were gathered around the man with the broken arm. Their boredom was broken. They had something to amuse them.

Lassiter passed the tower with its dropped signal board. He crossed the maze of tracks of the yard. At the far end were the roundhouse, the shops and the offices of the division superintendent. No one looked at him twice. They were used to bums. He sat down in the shade of an ore car that was shunted onto a siding, waiting to be moved up the branch line to one of the mines.

He pulled his hat over his eyes, leaned his elbows on his knees and went into a comatose rest that was not sleep. He was aware of what went on around him, but his mind was on the lake he had just crossed.

It had been pure hell. In twenty-five years of wandering across the land he had never gone through anything like it. The furnace heat. The relentless sun. The glare reflected against his burning eyeballs by the alkali crust. The crust itself, like skim ice, cracking under his weight, the knife sharp edges cutting at the old boots. The endless moving. Eighteen hours of constant walking. It was a nightmare that would live with him. He would keep it alive until he found answers. He had the questions.

Why had it been necessary? Why had he been singled out to die? Why had a man he barely knew set him up as a pigeon to hang for a killing he had not done?

He meant to find out. He had to find out. Was it sheer accident that he alone of the five had been captured and tried? Or had some enemy he didn't know about chosen this way to get rid of him? He had to know which if he meant to go on living. If he wasn't to spend his life suspecting every man and woman in it.

The mountains around the lake purpled into night. The stars came out and the lake surface shimmered in the deep glow. Two passenger trains, one going east, one west, made their scant call at the yellow station. Lassiter watched. He sat unmoving as a cat. The whiskey began to loosen the coiled nerves within him.

2

THE freight was carrying cattle. You could smell them in the hot air, hear their bellowing despair at being crammed into the racketing cars, their bellowing for water that no one gave them.

One of the cars had a hot box. Smoke was coming from the housing around the axle. There were a lot of lanterns bobbing in the dark yard, a lot of men, a lot of discussion. Then the train was ready to roll on. Lassiter looked at the sky and saw that it was after midnight.

He stood up. There was pain in his belly. It held nothing but the whiskey and water. He was in no hurry. The long train jerked, its couplings clanked down its length as the locomotive tried to drag it into motion.

When it was moving out he went

forward with a restored catlike grace, caught the handrail of the car just ahead of the caboose and swung himself to the step. He hung there, making no move to climb until they were well clear of the yard, snaking toward the pass through the mountains, heading west. It was going in the wrong direction. His direction was south.

He clawed to the top of the lurching car. The track was hastily, badly laid, the wheels were not entirely round. The couplings jarred, the train rocked, the cattle bawled. Ahead, the stream of sparks spewing from the bell stack as the stoker shoved in wood looked like a geyser fed from hell.

A shadow appeared from the caboose and climbed the ladder. Lassiter did not try to hide. There wasn't any place.

The freight conductor saw him and came along the catwalk, swaying easily with the jerking rhythm of the train. He carried a bullseye lantern in one hand, a short, heavy club in the other.

He made the jump from the caboose and advanced on Lassiter cautiously.

"What do you think you're doing here?"

"Riding," Lassiter said.

"Not on this railroad. The orders are to throw you bums off in the desert. That's why we don't bother you in town. Jump."

Lassiter looked down on the lake bed, hard, shining, white. He looked at the railroad man.

"I walked seventy miles across that. That's enough."

The man did not believe him. "Jump, or I'll knock you off."

Lassiter's shoulders moved in a helpless gesture. He started toward the ladder. He had almost reached it. The conductor was crowding him. Lassiter knew what would happen. As soon as he went down, had both hands on the top rung, the man would use his club against his knuckles.

Lassiter made a sudden twist. One hand reached out and caught the wrist

17

that held the club. He wrenched it and the stick fell to the car top and rolled away. His other hand grabbed the man's shirt. He jerked him from his feet and held him up, a struggling rabbit. He used his free hand to find the gun in the conductor's pocket. It was small, a thirty-two. He threw the man off the train. The train went on. In the starlight Lassiter saw the conductor land on the white lake and roll, then struggle to his feet and shake his fist, yelling. The yells faded and the jumping figure melted into the night.

Lassiter sat down on the catwalk. The air rushing at him was still hot, but it moved. It felt good. It felt good to sit quiet and watch the awful lake sweep by. Then the tracks veered away from it and the locomotive began the climb into the pass. The grade twisted, sharpened. The speed of the train slowed.

Lassiter climbed down the ladder. Two men played poker at the folding table in the caboose, playing with greasy cards, coins and a few crumpled bills between them. He guessed who they were, the punchers sent along with the cattle shipment to feed and water the animals. They had not bothered with the job in the hot sink of the Puente stop.

They did not look up as he opened the door and stepped in, clattering noise and a backwash of soot coming with him. The man with his back to the door spoke without turning.

"That took you long enough."

The second man looked up from the cards, saw the gun in Lassiter's hand and his mouth fell open. He tried to get words out and couldn't. His partner saw the expression and turned.

Lassiter said, "Hands on the table. All of them."

The men sat still. He allowed a fast glance around the cramped, swaying room. Four bunks built against one wall. A small wood stove, skillet, black coffee pot. The riders' gear, saddles, ropes, blanket rolls piled in one corner. Guns and belts lay on top of the pile.

The puncher facing him was close to Lassiter's size. He wore a hickory shirt, jeans nearly new, hand stitched boots. Lassiter particularly approved of the boots. He said, "Stand up," and watched the man rise.

"Strip."

The puncher's eyes bugged. "What?"

"Undress." Lassiter leveled the gun.

The man looked from the eye of the muzzle, up, into the two black eyes that directed it. Hastily he began to peel off his clothes.

"Out on the platform now. Jump."

The naked man stared. "Like this?"

"Like that. It's warm out."

"I'll be killed."

"We're only moving ten miles an hour. Out."

The puncher moved toward the door. Lassiter stepped to one side, waiting for him to make a grab for the gun. He didn't. He glared, and pulled the door open, went out, and hesitated on the windy, cinder strafed platform. Lassiter put his boots against the bare buttocks and pushed. The puncher went over the railing. He lit on the right of way, somersaulted and came up to his knees.

Lassiter's back was turned to the card table. He heard the chair scrape and faced around. The second man was on his feet, diving forward, hands widespread to wrap Lassiter in a bear hug.

Lassiter stepped inside the embrace. The light gun broke the puncher's nose, flattened the bridge, sent blood spurting downward. The gun wasn't heavy enough. It didn't knock the man out. In spite of the dazing pain the puncher came on, arms closing around Lassiter, momentum forcing him out to the platform.

Lassiter came up against the rail. For a moment they both swayed over it. The right lurch of the train would throw them both over. Instead, the next lurch favored Lassiter. He got his footing and brought his knee up full force into the crotch. The hurt bent the man forward, broke his hold.

Lassiter hit him three quick chops with the gun barrel. He opened one cheek, knocked teeth out of the gasping mouth, connected solidly with the temple. The man staggered back into the caboose, stumbled into the table and fell. Lassiter was on him, swinging the gun as the man tried to rise. The puncher collapsed and lay unconscious. Lassiter checked the swinging gun. Killing the puncher wouldn't buy him anything.

He stood getting his breath back, waiting for the strength to pick up the puncher and throw him off the train. He did not want a witness around to remember where he himself left the car.

Then he changed his mind. It was hard on a man in this land without a horse. He knew about walking. He took a coiled rope from a saddle horn, tied the man, set the table upright and shoved him under it, out of the way. If he came to, he could be knocked out again.

He kicked the door shut to cut out some of the racket, then checked the coffee pot. It was better than half full. Hot. He filled a battered cup from the shelf above the stove. The coffee sizzled against the spout of the pot. Lassiter poured it down his throat to the pain in his stomach. After the first gasp the heat helped.

There was a bottle of whiskey on the shelf, a quarter full. He drank half the cup of coffee, laced the rest and drank that. Then he peeled off the rank clothes that didn't fit and tossed them aside.

His skin was white where it had been protected from the sun. He stood naked before the piece of broken mirror tacked to the wall and used warm water from the pail, shaving with the conductor's razor. The blade broke the heat blisters around his straight lipped mouth. He looked worse than before,

23

as if someone had gone over him with a branding iron.

He washed, then dressed in the tall puncher's clothes. They fitted better than those he had taken from the man in Harmony.

That had been bad, but there had been no choice. Time had been short. They had built the scaffold in the town square, outside the jail, built it for use when his sentence came down from the judge. He had not seen it from the cell, but the noise of hammering had come around the corner and in at the jail window. Every day for two weeks.

He had hated that jail, but he had had to wait for his chance. They had watched him closely at first. And while he waited he listened to the talk in the corridor and in the sheriff's office beyond.

He heard the excitement when they brought in the man they'd found wandering around on the dry lake. He heard the man's babbling and

24

crying. Someone commented that the heat out there had driven him insane.

"Nobody ever crossed that lake and lived or kept his wits, that I know of." The sheriff was talking to the doctor, sounding certain. "Not on foot, that's for damn sure."

Lassiter remembered the lake when his chance finally came. For a week they kept an armed guard in the corridor. Then they tired of that and the sheriff took his pants and boots. They had a fine laugh. They agreed that a nearly naked man, barefoot, could not make a successful break.

It was then that he began to make a tool. On the first night he had found one metal spring strap of his bed broken. The ends were riveted to the angle iron frame. It took him two days, pushing the shorter piece up and down until the rivet snapped. Then he began sharpening the jagged end, rubbing it against the rough stone of the cell wall. He needed a gouge

25

to dig out the window frame around the bars. The wood was sun baked, weakened by dry rot, but not enough that he could pull the bars free.

The strap iron was the only tool he had hard enough to break the wood. He worked constantly, by the hour. By the day. At night. He rubbed until his arms ached, his fingers numbed.

It was slow going. The point was still not as sharp as he wanted, but he could wait no longer. The guard told him when he brought the supper plate of beans. Told him, grinning. The judge had passed the sentence. They were going to hang him first thing in the morning.

He had the night to work. He waited for the jail to quiet down. But tonight it didn't quiet. A hot poker game started in the front office. He did not know how many there were, but he heard at least seven voices. He sweat, waiting for the game to break up. It didn't. The night was going. Dawn came early in midsummer. The bastards meant to play through the night, until time for the hanging.

He moved to the window and dug at the bottom sill where the center bar was embedded. It resisted more than he had thought. It was frustrating. The weathered wood came out in little splinters, almost sawdust.

Panic chilled him. He fought that down. He worked harder.

He had a hole big enough to let him wiggle the bar. He dug a groove beside it, then took the bar in both hands and wrenched it out.

The hole was not big enough to let him slide through. He started on the next bar. The stars were paling and sweat muddied the dirt on the stone floor under his feet when the bar gave. He put down the pry, took the bar in both hands and lifted himself until his bare feet wedged against the sill. He used the leverage of his full weight, his full pressure against the low end of the bar. It gave grudgingly, teasing, holding, rusted in its place.

It came loose suddenly, surprising him. The sound of its tearing out sounded loud to him. He wasn't braced for the release. He slammed back. He hit on his back on the stones. The wind was knocked out of him. He lay gasping like a fish, holding tight to the bar. At least he had not dropped it. If the poker players hadn't heard the rending wood they surely would have heard the iron clank on the stones.

He listened for footsteps, looking at the window. He had to move, but he couldn't until he could breathe.

Laughter came from the front office. He filled his lungs and got up. His back hurt as he jumped to the window. The opening was still a tight squeeze, but it had to do. There was no more time. His undershirt tore. His skin was clawed by rust. He forced through, sidewise, standing the pain.

His buttocks burned on the iron. Then he fell headlong. He landed on his outstretched hands in the rubble of the alley. He rolled and got up, leaned tight against the wall, listened.

The laughter and voices of the game came through the window. He turned, searching for movement in the dark alley. A cat streaked by. Nothing more. His bare feet felt the way, dodging trash, broken glass, discarded peach cans with jagged lids twisted back.

He was cautious, listening for the warning rattle of a snake, hoping not to step on the furry wrath of a tarantula or a scorpion's upraised poison tail.

He reached the street corner. His impulse was to steal a horse. He saw two animals at the hitch rack two blocks away and no one was on the street. He could steal one and ride for the hills. But there would be pursuit as soon as the horse was missed. They knew the territory and its short cuts. He did not. Their chances of running him down were better than his were to get away, without pants, without boots, without a gun.

It was better to do the unexpected. He was alive because that was his pattern, to do the thing another man would not.

The idea of the lake beckoned. It was beyond the hill, but his mind saw its flat surface shining in the fading night. If it were like other dry lakes in the country it would be baked hard, windswept, clear of dust. A man's steps would not leave an imprint to follow.

It lay to the north, opposite to the direction he wanted to go. But there was a railroad. If he could cross the lake. If he could find the railroad.

First he needed boots. He needed pants, a shirt, a hat. He heard footsteps on the wooden sidewalk, staggering, coming toward him from the saloon.

The short man stepped into the intersection of the alley. Lassiter had him by the throat before he knew that anyone was there, wheeling him into the alley's mouth. He gave one helpless, frightened bleat and then went down into the dust as the iron fingers choked him unconscious.

30

The pants were too short, but the waist was big enough to go around Lassiter's flat hips. The hat did fit. The boots were too tight. He barely got them on.

3

LASSITER sat on the floor of the rocking caboose with a wash basin, facing the door, working on his blistered feet.

He soaked them, washed them carefully, bled the blisters with a knife tip slid beneath the outer skin to leave the lifted sacks unbroken. Always he took important care of his feet. Even when it was impossible to wash the rest of his body. A man's life often could depend on his feet.

He rifled the bedrolls and found clean socks and eased them on. They were tight enough to serve as bandages. So far he was doing fine. The new pants fitted surprisingly well. So did the shirt. Both hats were too small, he would have to keep the short man's. The hand stitched boots, he held his breath on the boots.

He was relieved that they slid on easily. They might be a trifle loose normally, but on his swollen feet it was all to the good.

He stood up, stepping down, testing them, satisfied. He felt in the pockets of the pants. There was a twenty dollar gold piece. Lassiter came as close to smiling as he had in a long time.

He gathered the coins and bills from the table, chose the better of the two guns and fastened the belt around his waist, noting with approval that is loops were well filled.

Hunger growled in his empty belly. He turned to the larder box. He found salt meat, eggs, cooked beans, cold biscuits. He put meat in the skillet on the stove, added eggs and beans. After he had eaten he finished the bottle of whiskey.

The train whistled. Lassiter looked out of the small window. They were running now through the mountains. The sky in the east was beginning to gray.

He turned back to finish the coffee, wished there was more whiskey, and looked. He found none. He did find a flour sack, nearly empty, wrapped what food was left in the larder in a red handkerchief and put it in with the flour. He tied the sack, wrapped it in one of the bedrolls, selected the better saddle, made certain the rope looped to its horn was good, took a look at the cowboy under the table. The puncher was still out but his breathing was regular. Lassiter moved him, tied him to a leg of the stove. If he came to he could not get up without tipping the stove on top of himself. He would not be at the window to see when Lassiter left the train.

The air was cooler on top of the rocking car, fresher, less burdened than that in the sweltering caboose. It was welcome in spite of the constant rain of smoke and cinders that swept back from the laboring engine.

He had not slept for over forty-eight hours, but even the whiskey hadn't made him sleepy. He sat with the saddle, and bedroll at his side, leaning on it, and watched the line of hills walling in the throat of the pass, cutting out the lower stars behind their sharp peaks.

The train inched up the winding grade. He could have walked faster. It ran finally through a cut so narrow that it made an open tunnel. Then the engine dipped down and the speed increased. From his perch Lassiter saw the rusting hulks of other locomotives that had failed to make the sharp cutbacks, had left the tracks on this stretch of rail.

After dawn they dropped into a long valley, running west. The complexion of the country changed as the mountain range fell behind. Here was more moisture, streams bridged by wooden trestles, cattle in small bunches in the side draws. The headquarters buildings of several ranches made uneven sprawls in the far distance across the rolling lowlands ahead.

He did not dare approach one of these, but if he could spot an isolated line camp . . . he had to have a horse. He watched the lifting ground of the line of hills the train paralleled, the south border of the valley.

It was better than an hour before he saw it, a single room cabin on the bench a quarter of a mile above the right of way. No smoke came from the tin stack, but he saw the moving bulk of horses in the pole corral.

The train was now running better than twenty miles an hour. He pitched the saddle and bedroll over the edge and dropped down the handrails to the bottom of the ladder and watched his chance. The tracks followed a manmade embankment, a manmade ditch beside it. The ditch was a foot deep in matted grass. Ahead there was a small, rising grade.

Lassiter timed his jump for the moment when the grade would cut down the speed. He dropped away, running as he landed, letting his momentum rush him toward the bottom of the ditch. The stretch of his flying steps was not enough. He lost his balance and plunged headlong. The grass broke his fall but the air was driven out of him. He lay face down, relaxing, waiting for the convulsion of breathing to pass.

He got up, not looking after the train, and walked back along the ditch to the saddle and bedroll. He slung the roll over his shoulder, caught up the saddle, crossed the right of way and climbed the bench towards the line camp.

The cabin was of logs, the bark left on. It had a sod roof, a single window. There was no one outside, but three horses stood head down in the corral. One was saddled.

He had hoped the place would be empty, that the horses were left there as relays for the line rider who might be at the far end of his swing. But a rider would not go off and leave a horse saddled.

He became careful. He dropped the gear on the shadow of the corral fence and walked toward the cabin. Slow. He kept his hand away from the holstered gun. He did not want anyone watching through the window to think he was hostile.

There was no challenge. He saw no movement at the window. He came around the corner of the building and found the door ajar. He stopped, puzzled. He had been in plain view for half an hour. The saddled horse did not make sense if the line rider was simply sleeping late. Where was he?

Lassiter came against the door silently, lifting his gun with his right hand, pushing the slab door inward with the muzzle. The hinges made no sound.

He looked at the dim interior and for a moment thought it was empty. Then he saw movement in the lower bunk across the room. His eyes adjusted to the light. He saw the tangle of a naked man, thrashing heavily. At first he thought the man was alone, fighting loneliness. Then he saw the woman under him.

Lassiter slipped the gun into its holster and stepped inside. He was not seen. He sat down in the chair beside the door.

The woman seemed inexperienced but trying hard. The man was rough, careless of her, artless, a pile driver. He held her pinioned and beat out his need. Then he was spent and rolled away. The woman's cry was high.

"Clint. Don't leave me up here like this. I almost . . . "

The man was on his back, his voice heavy, smug, mocking. "Sorry, Ma'am. It's all gone. Finish off yourself."

She flung herself up, rocking, swinging her feet to the floor, taut as a bowstring. Her head snapped up as she saw the man quiet in the chair. A gasp choked from her. The sound brought Clint upright suddenly. Fright and fury started him cursing.

"Who the hell are you? What do you want here?"

"A horse."

"Get the devil out of here." Clint looked towards his clothes, jumbled on the table, the gun beside them.

Lassiter looked too. The clothes said cowhand. The dress on the chair had cost too much. It said rancher's daughter, or wife. Lassiter took out his gun. He stood up and walked forward, between the table and the bunk. The woman tried to rise. Clint grabbed her, pulled her back against him as a shield.

When Lassiter was close enough he reached across the woman and swung the gun barrel against the side of Clint's head. The man let go of the woman, rolled over to the floor. He was heavier than Lassiter. He crouched to charge and came in low. Lassiter's boot toe caught him under the chin. The head went up, the body after it. He went over backward and sat down hard. He was not out, but he was too dazed to move again. Lassiter saw no need to hurry. He found a rope coiled on a peg against the wall, tied Clint's ankles and wrists together and left him sitting, glass eyed.

The women lay back as Clint had thrown her, a handsome figure. Except for the wide worry in her eye she looked like a painting hanging over a San Franscisco bar. Reclining nude with pearls. She didn't have pearls. Lassiter stood looking down, admiring her. He had been in jail for four weeks.

"You didn't get a fair shake from Clint," he said, and took off his clothes.

He sat down on the bed and she recoiled, looking at the raw, red blisters on his face. He smiled at her.

"Don't worry. It's only sunburn."

He touched her shoulder, drew his hand down the velvet back with gentle pressure. It did not take long. She was already on the road. There was a little time while she stayed within herself as if not quite believing what was happening. Then she came out, and they made up for what they had missed.

41

When he got up she put out a hand to hold him, but it had no strength. It fell back and lay limp.

"God," she said.

The tone was the absolute thanksgiving. He nodded, and reached for his pants.

"You ought to be hungry by now. Get up, get us some breakfast."

She watched him, unmoving, holding onto the moment that was past. Then slowly she sat up, as if she were dreaming. Her voice had a dream quality.

"My name is Laura. Do you want a job?"

"I've got a job."

"Around here?"

"Not here. I'm looking for a man."

Her smile flashed, strong and fresh. "So was I. My husband would hire you. He's a good man to work for. He pays his people well."

"So do you. What's wrong with him?"

She stood up quickly. She had a

straight, firm body, a proud carriage.

"Mind your tongue. Build a fire if you want to eat. Bring some water from the well."

He finished dressing, buckled on the gun belt and built the fire, picked up a pail and went outside. He came back with the pail on one hand, his gun in the other. Laura might have taken up Clint's gun or untied the cowhand. The man had come out of his daze.

She had done neither. She had her clothes on and stood in the middle of the room, combing her long, honey colored hair through her fingers, winding it in a prim knot low on her neck.

When it was fastened she stood on a chair and reached down the ham butt that hung from a rafter, put it on the table and took a long knife from the drawer.

"I'll do that." He took the knife from her. He did not like knives in other people's hands.

He sliced the meat while she made

coffee. Then he wiped the blade, stuck the knife in his belt and sat down to watch her at the stove. She was worth watching, direct, efficient, a paragon of virtures, even a good cook.

She served the two of them and sat with him, eating with good appetite. Afterward he brought in his flour sack and she added the ham, a string of jerked meat and some coffee to the small store.

He looked around the room, considering whether he needed anything else from it. She lifted herself on tiptoe and raised her mouth for his parting kiss. Like an old married couple starting the day. He kissed her absently. There was one more thing to take along. He drew his gun and handed her the knife.

"Cut Clint loose and throw him his clothes."

She sounded relieved. "You'll take him with you?"

"I don't want him putting people on my trail. You . . . I don't think you'll remember any of us were here."

"Not likely." She cut the rope while Lassiter stood where he had a clear shot even if the man tried again to use her as shield. "Clint, whose word do you think they'd take at the ranch, yours or mine? If you ever come near there again I'll have you killed."

Clint's eyes showed that he believed her. Under the gun he fought into his clothes, carried his saddle out, caught up the horses in the corral and threw his gear and Lassiter's on the animals, and climbed onto one.

Laura tied his legs, passing the rope under the animal's belly, and tied his hands to the pommel. She started toward the third horse.

Lassiter said, "No."

Her brows went up. "You're not stranding me here?"

"How far is it to the ranch?"

"Five miles."

"I've walked further. You can make it. I need the time to get clear. Just in case." He stepped to the saddle and ran lead lines from the other animals.

Laura, flushed now with helpless anger, made a more beguiling picture than ever. Lassiter looked back once and found her still watching. Then he turned his train up the hillside and rode south.

He was over the crest by noon, heading into an area of badlands. He pulled up, got down, freed Clint, holding his gun ready and watched the man drop to the ground. The cowhand's eyes were murderous.

"Goodbye, Clint. Remember what the lady said about the ranch. I'll be back. I'll know if you've been foolish."

"Damn you. What are you . . . put a man afoot out here?"

"A busy man."

Lassiter climbed to the saddle again, pulled Clint's horse in behind and rode south. An hour later he drew up in a small, bleak valley. He had seen no cattle on this side of the ridge, but he did not know what lay ahead. He studied the brand on the horses' flanks. A triangle. That had to be changed. He could run into a rider who knew the brand. He had no intention of hanging as a horse thief. But he did not have a running iron.

He turned two animals loose and lashed the other against two trees, forelegs tied to one, rear legs to the other. He got the conductor's razor from the blanket roll and shaved a pattern in the horse's hair, a second triangle laid over the first, tilted so that the two formed a six pointed star.

He built a smokeless fire and laid the knife from the line camp in the glowing embers. When it was red hot he seared the flesh exposed by the shaving, puckering the skin, curling the edges of the bordered hair. The horse thrashed. He swung the barrel of the forty-five against its jaw. It stood quivering but steady as he finished the burning.

It was crude, but it had to do. He cut fat from the ham and rubbed it

47

into the burn to keep the flies from the raw sore. He kicked the fire out, untied the horse, mounted and rode south.

Toward evening he followed a game trail to a seep spring, got down, drank, watered the horse. He wet the animal's blistered flank and rubbed mud across the brand and down the leg. When it dried it made a cake, blurring the new brand.

He mounted again and rode south.

4

THE room was cramped, narrow, mean. It held a bed, a washstand with bowl and pitcher, the pitcher chipped, the bowl cracked. Debbie was sitting in the bed, leaning back on both arms braced rigid behind her. She had been asleep. This was how she had come up when his shoulder crashed against the door. Moonlight, soft and kind, lighted her. The fright in her eyes glowed.

Lassiter used his boot to kick the splintered door shut. He crossed and stuck a match against the wick of the bracketed lamp. She had not moved when he turned to her. The cover clung tight over her flaccid stomach. The nightgown pulled tight, down from her brown neck.

From the side of the bed he looked on her. He had not shaved in five days since he had left the train. His black beard was patchy, pushing around the scabs over the blisters. His gaunted cheeks were peeling.

"Where is he?"

Her round face held shock. The shock of seeing a ghost. His ghost.

"Lassiter? Lassiter. You're alive. You didn't hang?"

"You knew I was to hang?"

She swallowed, as if that would take back the words. Trying to cover them she hurried.

"I didn't mean . . . "

His swinging hand drove the voice back into her throat with a slap across the red mouth.

"Where's Elkhorn?"

Tears budded and broke. Fright made her pretty face ugly. He reached for the cover, stripped it away, hurled it toward a corner. She crouched back.

"Please. Please. I'd tell you if I knew . . . "

His fingers tangled in the neck of her gown, hauled on it. He meant to yank her to her feet. Instead, the cloth ripped. The gown tore away in his hand.

Already keyed up by his dull burning rage, he responded to her nakedness. Anger did this to him. Women did this to him. It made him angrier. It made him vulnerable.

He knew now that in the beginning she had offered herself to him on Elkhorn's order. She offered now in terror, to save her life. He read it in the change in her eyes. Behind the fear came cunning, the scheming of a cat.

He threw the gown at her face, bent, locked both hands around her throat. Her body convulsed. He held her tight. He would not break her neck, but she did not know this. She expected death. He meant to have control. She choked and he flung her back into the pillow.

"Lassiter," Her voice was bruised, the word slurred. The tawny throat kept the red imprint of his fingers. She covered them with her hand. "I don't know where he is. I don't." Her pitch rose, broke in a cry. "I'd tell you. I'd tell you. Even if they killed me for it. I'd tell you."

"Who would kill you?"

Her wild eyes darted to the single window. He sprang to it and looked out. There were no one. He came back.

"Who?"

She leaned towards him, a finger lifted in caution, whispering. "Don Miguel. Somebody from him. You know that, Lassiter."

He did know. And now he knew that he couldn't find Elkhorn through her. For probably the first time she was telling him the truth.

"So Elkhorn works for Miguel."

"Everybody here does, when he sends for them."

"You too?"

"I have to live. This is a bad place. I hate it."

"What's keeping you here?"

"I can't get away. They'd find me. You can't get away either unless you

52

go now." She became urgent. "Lassiter, you were good to me, before. Better than any man ever was. I want to pay you back. All I can do is warn you. Go away. Now. Before they know you've been here."

"Pay me back with the truth about Elkhorn."

She nodded, reached for his shirt and pulled him toward her, down to sit on the bed.

"I don't know where he went. He came back after the holdup and said you were caught. He said they'd hang you. He was told to hide out until you were dead. He went away. That same night. Lassiter?"

This close to her he smelled her ripe want, the hot sourness. She lay back, her legs opening, her breasts dull gold, big as melons. He put his hand on her stomach, bending above her.

"What's the rest of it? He set you on me. What did he say? *Get me another man*, or *Get me Lassiter?*"

"You, by name." He said, "Tell him

53

the bank is easy, we can't miss. Tell him you'll be waiting when he gets back."

"Why me? He didn't know me. I hadn't been in this town a month."

She lifted her shoulders against the pillow.

"Frame up." Absently he rubbed at her, the way he would fondle the hair of a dog, thinking back, talking to himself, not her. "They never meant to rob that bank. They didn't take the money. They shot the banker and rode out. Left me to hang for it. Why would Elkhorn want me hung?"

A rhetorical question. She wouldn't know. She was not in their confidence. He looked at her anyway. She was no longer concerned with questions and answers. He was.

It was a frame. What she had said made that plain. Who was behind it? Who wanted him hung for murder? Some secret enemy hating him out of the past, willing to go to big trouble to see him dead? He had to know.

Without an answer, he would never be secure again. His back would always be a target.

She took his hand, cradling it. He moved it up, spread the fingers around her neck again, shook her head until her eyes opened, focused.

"Will Elkhorn come back to see you?"

She made a face of misery. "He always does."

"I'll wait."

The eyes widened. "Here?"

"No. Across the street."

"He might send a messenger. You wouldn't know him."

"Will you signal me? Throw a towel out of the window?"

The cunning showed again. "Afterwards will you get me away from here?"

"Yes."

"I'll help you. Now . . ." Her hands went to his shirt, pulling at the buttonholes.

He undressed, blew out the light and

went back to the bed, sank into the cumulous mounds of her breasts. Since the woman in the camp line his hunger had been fierce. It flamed now. Was it strength or weakness, this need of woman? There was much danger here, he knew.

She was asleep when he left the room in the bright morning. He crossed the street and took his old room at the Casa del Orillo, the upstairs corner room that looked down on the row of cribs in the alley. On Debbie Dean's door. From that room he had first seen her in front of her door, beckoning him down.

He stripped and washed, the water in the pitcher hot from sitting where the sun struck it. The dust that came off him turned the water the color of blood, thick as soup, and left an inch of sediment in the bowl. He soaked the crust from his healed blisters, shaved trimmed his hair. The clothes he had taken from the puncher on the train he threw out of the window. He opened the suitcase he had left at the Casa when he went north, pried up the false bottom. The money belt had not been found. It was there. He put it around his waist, dressed in his own clothes. Clean, he looked like a gambler, choosy about his dress, particularly the soft tanned deerskin boots.

He pulled the table and chair into the corner where the two windows met and sat down to watch. From the alley window he could see what men Debbie entertained. From the other he had a view of the town.

Across the main street of Orillo the States and Mexico faced each other. The larger section of the double town lay south of the boundary line.

A lot of men found it a convenient headquarters. There was little law in any case, but if trouble came a man need only cross the road to be in another country, where those wanting him had no jurisdiction. It made the town popular. Mexicans outnumbered Americans on the north side and there were more Yankees in the community south of the border. All of them were wanted in their own country.

Orillo was not handsome. The street was wide enough, with the Mexican influence of the plaza in the middle, but years of traffic, horses' hoofs and wheels had dug it into a river of fine dust. The wooden sidewalk, two feet above the road, wasn't high enough to escape the silt piled in corduroy ridges, blown up by the hot winds at night and never kicked quite clear during the day. The buildings south of the line were 'dobe mud baked into bricks and laid up, plastered with more mud. When they had first been built they were washed with a lime based mix in garish blues and pink. The surfaces had flaked away, left the walls blotched like liver spots on an old man's hands.

On the American side the structures were frame, board and batten, and no one had ever bothered to paint them. Raw wood, the sun had soaked the moisture and life out of them. Nails fell out, battens curled away, boards bulged and bent. You could look through the walls at whatever went on inside. There was no privacy.

There was no privacy in the town. There was no streets behind the square, only radiating alleys like the spokes of a wheel, letting onto desert. Life was lived in full view. Upstairs, Lassiter watched it.

At the table he ate the food the Mexican cook brought up to him. He played solitaire. He watched the guests that went into Debbie's crib. One of these would be Elkhorn or a messenger from Elkhorn.

Elkhorn was not the man's name. Lassiter did not know what the real one was. No one he had talked to admitted knowing. Few people in Orillo used their own names. He had heard the story when he was here before. The man had arrived one night, an elk's horn tied to his saddle. He'd opened a saloon below the Casa and hung the horn over the back bar. When a customer asked his name he had pointed at the horn. He did not own the bar now. He had sold it two years before Lassiter had found the town. But he was still called Elkhorn.

Lassiter waited, and thought about the man, thought about the holdup, step by step.

Debbie had sent him to Elkhorn. Elkhorn had told him about the bank. "There'll be five of us," Elkhorn said. "It will be easy."

It had been too easy. He should have been suspicious then. They had ridden into Harmony at nine-thirty in the morning, passed the bank, turned in at the livery next door. They tied up the barn man in his office, left one man in the runway with the horses. Elkhorn and two men went toward the front door of the bank. Lassiter was sent down the alley to the rear. At exactly ten o'clock he pushed the door open. He saw Elkhorn's group come in the front. The bank president's desk was at the right of the front door. He stood

60

up as they came in. Without a word Elkhorn shot him. Twice.

The shooting wasn't necessary. The banker didn't have a gun. He gave no sign that he suspected them. Elkhorn shot and they turned and ran out of the door. They did not try for any money. Lassiter stood in confusion, then turned and jumped back to the alley. Three men dropped from the bank roof, knocked him flat. By the time he was wrestled to his feet the sheriff and two deputies had him under their guns.

That was the moment when Elkhorn's crowd broke from the barn. Elkhorn yelled at him. "We'll be back for you." Then they wheeled down the alley, ducking low in the saddles. A few wild shots followed them. Then they were gone. Lassiter was bulldozed to the cell. He was convicted of the murder.

He had not expected Elkhorn to break him out. He had expected to find him at his ease in Orillo. He believed Debbie's word that Elkhorn was hiding out. But sooner or later Elkhorn would contact her. There was some strong tie between them. It was not love. It could be Don Miguel.

Lassiter waited ten days. Elkhorn did not come. No towel was thrown out of Debbie's window. He could not wait forever. He went to see Don Miguel.

He had seen the fat man once before. On his first night in town the Mexican woman who ran the Casa had told him. "You want to stay in Orilla, you see Don Miguel. You don't see him, you don't stay. Not alive." The Don had put it differently, outlining the rules by which the town was run. "I will tolerate no killing in Orilla, Senor. If a man is wanted dead, it is arranged to happen elsewhere."

He had heard the name increasingly as he moved across the country. First in the north, in the capital at Prescott. Riding south, he heard it in Tucson. From Juarez along the border to San Luis. In the stories of stolen cattle and stolen gold the words, 'the fat man' came up. Among the Chinese of the mining camps it was mentioned in connection with opium. Among the women he was called the slaver.

He found a pattern, a web laid across the border area and running south, deep into the Sierra Madres. From those around the Clantons, Curly Bill 'Brocius,' whose name was not Brocius, around Ringo, he heard growls over tribute paid to move their rustled cattle out of Mexico into the States.

He heard about the massacre at Skeleton Canyon, a Mexican smuggling train ambushed below the Devil's Kitchen. Six men killed there, the skeletons of the pack mules scattered across the rolling land below the canyon mouth. The story said the Mexicans had tried to double-cross Don Miguel, that the fat man had set the outlaws on the train. How much of the ninety-thousand dollars in gold and silver that the Mexicans were taking home was lost, how much flowed along the web to Don Miguel was not known.

Whatever moved in that land made the web tremble back to its center in Orillo. It was a land of bleak mountains, sandy, waterless waste, blood, terror, death. Governor Wallace had complained to the President that there was not an honest dollar made in the whole territory, not an honest man to make it.

Lassiter went to see Don Miguel this second time. The sun was hot, the dust in the windy air stifling. Both sides of the plaza dozed. Men lay with their hats over their eyes in the shade of the cottonwoods, squatted under the wooden awnings. All of them knew when Lassiter came out of the Casa, walked into the street. He dodged a dragging burro train, crossed to the long mud wall faced by the fence of occatillo and sahuaro, stopped before the iron grille gate.

Beyond the gate the guard lolled in the patio. His black eyes stared out at Lassiter without expression.

Lassiter said, "Don Miguel," pushed hard against the gate, forced it inward, forced the guard back. The guard shook his head. "He says not to let you in,"

"I'm in."

There was a long blade knife in the man's belt. His hand caught the hilt, pulling it upward.

"Get out."

Lassiter paused, shrugged as if in resignation, half turned away. He snapped back. His hand clamped on the knife wrist. He spun the guard, wrenched, yanked the shoulder out of joint, shoved the guard forward.

The guard screamed, clutched at the shoulder, tried to set it, failed and screamed again. Lassiter took the knife from the man's belt, flipped it over the wall into the cactus fence, walked around the guard and into the house.

Don Miguel sat at the black oak trestle table in the main hall. His chair was huge, thick arms and back, thick woven seat of cowhide strips. He needed it. He filled it. He weighed three hundred and fifty pounds. He was eating frijoles, his elbows like melting hams splayed on the board. He used corn tortillas to shovel the beans and sauce into a mouth like a purse.

Lassiter ducked under the beams of the low ceiling. The room was gray dark. Light slitted through unglazed openings in the three foot thick 'dobe wall. There was no other chair. Don Miguel's guests did not sit in his presence. The fat man did not look up.

Lassiter said, "Your guard needs a doctor. He tried to keep me out."

The fat man did not speak. He shoveled greedily until the pottery bowl was empty, cleaned it with a wipe of the last tortilla, snapped the purse mouth shut on the bite.

"Lassiter." The fat man licked his lips clean, the very red lips of a churlish baby. Bunching red flesh gathered to bury his eyes. "Lassiter, yes. So you hurt my guard."

"I hurt him."

The big shoulders lifted, dropped. "You now. You came here two months ago, said you wanted to stay. Heard the law. You rode north with Elkhorn. You had trouble. What do you want now?"

"Elkhorn."

"Why?"

"I'm going to kill him. He did his damndest to get me hung."

The fat man shrugged. "You didn't hang."

"Through no fault of his."

Don Miguel belched. "Why come to me?"

"You know where he is. He works for you."

The big flesh shook like a custard. The man chuckled. "Mucho hombre, Lassiter. You're not afraid, talking like that to me?"

"Not until you're afraid of me. Where is he?"

The red lips grinned. "You think I will give you a man you say works for me?"

67

"Not give. Sell."

Lassiter took a handkerchief from his pocket, unwrapped it, shoved the chili bowl out of the way, fanned fifty twenty dollar gold pieces in front of the fat man.

The little eyes disappeared within the flesh. The voice was pleased.

"Yes."

The fat man put a thick finger in his bulbous nose, tipped his head.

"You want him killed. Yes?"

"I want him killed no. I want to carve some answers out of him first."

The Don chuckled again. He did not touch the gold.

"Not enough for a good man."

"You get another thousand when I have him. Alive."

The eyes lifted, met Lassiter's. "Mucho hombre. Mucho hombre."

Lassiter turned his back, left the gold on the table, left the house.

5

TIME crowded him. A week. One week now and no word from Don Miguel. Given the chance that the fat man did not know where Elkhorn was, he should have learned by now. The grapevine of his organization should have pinpointed him.

Lassiter lay without his shirt, on the hot bed in the hot room. His eyes followed a tarantula walking upside-down on the rough, crumbling ceiling. Had he figured the fat man wrong? Would the Don keep the gold, let him lie here and sweat until he gave up and pulled out? The thought made him impatient.

He stood up, prowled the room, poured tequila from a warm bottle into a warm glass, turned toward the alley window, looked down on Debbie's door. He stopped the glass halfway to his lips.

A man had turned the corner, was walking down the alley. He was not Elkhorn. He was not from Elkhorn. He was more important. He was Sidney Blood. Wells Fargo.

He was tired of Blood. Blood always behind him. From border to border. From the river to the coast. A vulture shadow that stalked him. Blood, a company man professionally resenting whoever posed a threat against the Agency. No longer professional about Lassiter. Long ago it had swelled into a personal vendetta between them. There was that in the chemisty of the two. They would have been enemies if Lassiter had never touched a strongbox, never stopped a stage or train. A bond stronger than love cuffed them together. Deep respect. Deep hatred.

The glass in Lassiter's hand broke. He dropped it, did not look down. Blood in Orillo. It told him more about the fat man. No special agent could have come within miles of Orillo without Miguel's knowing it. So Don Miguel would deal with the private police.

It was no new discovery that Wells Fargo would deal with the Don Miguels of the West. To guard the treasure shipments the company would deal with Hell. An octopus in a disguise of respectability. Strangle any competition. Raid, beat down, compromise, drive out the little outfits. Kill them. Take over. Lassiter's rage affair with Wells Fargo was the one luxury emotion he allowed himself.

Blood went into the first crib, a short visit. He came out, went to the next, came out, went through Debbie Dean's door. Blood looking for someone. Looking for Lassiter.

Lassiter left the window, poured another drink, threw it down his throat, waited while its heat spread. He put on his shirt. He looked at the gun in the belt hanging on the nail. Blood was dangerous even in Orillo. Single minded, bullheaded dangerous. Smart. Cool. But possessed by his mission.

Lassiter left the gun in the room, went down the stairs, through the side door into the alley.

Blood was standing over Debbie, sitting in a chair in a wrapper, scared. He swung as Lassiter pushed the door lightly open, dropped his shoulders in a quick crouch, stopped his spread fingered hand just short of the hip, an instinctive move. Lassiter's smile was thin. Blood knew the rules here, must have been here before. Even Blood did not go armed in Orillo.

"Looking for me, Sidney?" He weighted the name.

Blood straightened elaborately. Lassiter watched him put his face back together, cover his shock. It was sheer pleasure to watch the hunger, the victory that glinted in the light eyes retreat and die. Blood's voice was over controlled, hoarse.

"Yes, I'm looking for you. I'm taking you back."

Lassiter eased the door closed with his heel. "I'd think you'd get tired trying. You've had me in jail three times now. I didn't stay. I don't stay in jails. You've never convicted me yet."

Blood's eyes glowed again. "You're convicted this time. They'll hang you in Harmony. You'll be out of our way then."

"Sidney, I didn't kill that banker."

"I'm suppose to believe *that*?"

"Believe it. I didn't shoot him. I didn't have to. I don't kill people I don't have to."

"Not important. You're convicted. You'll hang. That's all I want. I couldn't nail you on that Colorado train holdup or the casino cleanout in San Francisco or the Angel's Camp stage robbery, but the Harmony sheriff's got you cold. He'll be glad to have you back. I'll be glad to give you to him."

"Seven years you've been trying, Sidney. What makes you so sure now?"

Blood judged the space between

them. They had fought before. Blood had won once. His lips pulled back. He had strong, white teeth.

"I'm sure."

"You working with the Mexican law now?"

Blood's head snapped sidewise. "All I have to do is get you one step across that street. I can bulldoze you that far."

"In Orillo? You touch me in this town, you'll never cross any street again. You know that."

Blood fought his temper. Lassiter had always baited him.

"You're on the wrong side of the line, Sidney. Wells Fargo isn't the law here. You're in Don Miguel's private kingdom. He's got a lot of muscle. Ask him."

Blood's eyes sparkled. "Maybe I already have."

Lassiter laughed at him. "You're losing your touch, Sidney. You're lying."

Blood reddened. He swept his hat

from the bed, walked at Lassiter. Lassiter opened the door, held it while Blood passed him, closed the door behind him. He did not have to watch where Blood went. He knew.

Across the room the girl found her voice. "Don Miguel will sell you out. You'd better ride."

"I want Elkhorn."

"You're crazy. If that man wants you, if he's from Wells Fargo . . . Lassiter . . . they're worse than any sheriff. They go everywhere, cross county lines, cross state lines, never give up. He can buy you from Miguel."

Lassiter's lips turned down. "He won't sell me here. He can't afford to. He made the rules, he has to keep them. People come because they're safe here. He keeps them safe. If he gave me to Blood his town would empty out in one hour. And somebody's gun would find him."

★ ★ ★

Don Miguel was saying the same thing, spreading his hands earnestly.

"I can't do it, Senor Blood. Why do you come asking me to commit suicide?"

"I didn't know he was your man."

"He isn't. But he has my sanctuary. If I give him to you who will trust me again? Who will do my work?"

Blood dug a folded poster from his pocket, spread it on the table, read it aloud, softly.

WANTED FOR MURDER
LASSITER
FIVE THOUSAND DOLLARS
REWARD

The Don's tongue went around the red lips. Blood brushed the paper towards him.

"You can have it all. Just shove the bastard across the line."

The fat man fondled the paper, ran it through his fingers as if it were money. Blood's word was good. He had done business with the agent before. They would do business again. He sounded thoughtful, a distance in his voice.

"Not in Orillo. Never in Orillo."

"Then get him out of Orillo. You must have some way to smoke him out."

The fat man folded his hands, sank back in the big chair. "Five thousand dollars. Why is he worth so much?"

"He's a devil. He's given us more trouble than anybody else west of the river. He plays with us like he was playing one of his damn chess games."

Blood's color was up, his fingers white around the chair arms, his voice explosive. Don Miguel took note. His eyes lidded. His interest did not show.

"He plays chess? What else is there about him? What's his history?"

Blood made the effort, quieted himself. Impatient, he chose to fight it by dragging the story out, going clear back.

"Family had money in Kentucky before the war. He enlisted with the

Confederates, fifteen years old, fought through to Lee's surrender. Drifted west then, tied in with the border raiders, the wild ones that wouldn't give up. He was driven out of Missouri, went to Colorado and started a stage line. Went broke. He's been holding up stages, trains, banks ever since. I can't prove it, but I know he must have taken half a million dollars."

The fat man touched his ear. "One would think that was enough to retire on. He had a reason other than money to keep active. No? Could Wells Fargo have been of injury to his stage line?"

Blood lifted one shoulder, showing disdain. "Every jerk mule skinner yells that the company put him out of business when he can't make it go. This one has a grudge because his partner killed himself when the banks closed down on them."

Don Miguel sighed. "Such a familiar pattern in these parts. But he is a cut above the average. He has, you say, played chess with a formidable organization, avoided your checkmate. He has strengths. What are his weaknesses?"

"Women. Are you going to give him to me or not?"

"Slowly, Senor. I like to know the value of what I sell . . . or buy. Go over to the American Hotel and wait. I will think on what is the best use of this man."

6

SIDNEY BLOOD, sitting under the gallery roof of the clapboard ramshackle that called itself the American Hotel, made the waiting less a burden. Lassiter had a little more to think about. Blood had been there for three days. Obviously the Don had not given him permission to take Lassiter in town. Perhaps then, Blood was waiting around on his own. Waiting for Lassiter's nerves to drive him to make a break.

Lassiter's patience was running thin. The change in the weather was partly responsible. The heat had increased. The air lay thick, not stirring, charged with static electricity. To the south heavy cloud banks climbed above the mountains, slow, cumbrous, laborious.

His try at buying Elkhorn from the Don had not worked. He was out a thousand dollars. He was blocked by Blood from going north. If he went south, Mexico was a hell of a big place in which to find one man who did not want to be found.

He had been sleeping in Debbie Dean's shack. Four hours a night. There were no locks on the rooms at the Casa. He did not intend that Blood should surprise him with a visit in the night, murder him and slip away. Blood, he thought, might be reaching the point of frustration where he would risk some such blunder. Even though it would cost him Don Miguel's help in any future transaction. It was time to make a move.

He packed his gear, called down the stair well to the woman who ran the Casa that he wanted to settle his bill. He went to the window, watched the copper colored urchin run out of the door, down the street. The woman took her time. The boy came back. She came up the stairs, swaying with the effort of lifting the burden of her

81

hips, her huge breasts. She counted the coins he dropped into the pink palm, her smile fawning.

"There is also a message from *him*. He wants to see you before you go."

Was that it? Had the fat man waited, testing him? He followed the woman down the stairs, a knot in his stomach. He did not look toward Blood, in the chair on the gallery across the plaza. He knew the agent watched him. Every eye on the street marked his passage.

The mozo in the patio led him past the main door, down the colonnade to its end, where the building turned a corner, made an ell. The room there was lighted by a window letting on the patio, over a work table that held carving tools.

In the middle of the room was a table, five feet square, better than waist high, its top a chess board of inlaid, fine grained blocks of wood, ebony and something almost white. Between the blocks ran bands of gold. The pattern was encased in a border of a wood that glowed iridescent in peacock colors, the joinings all but invisible. Magnificently crafted. Beyond the table Don Miguel sat in a chair on tall, thick legs.

Lassiter crossed the room, stopped at the table, looked at the chess pieces already set up on the square. They were at manzanita, one set in the dark blood red of the natural bark, oiled and rubbed to a high patina. The opposing set cleaned of bark, white, highly polished. None of the pieces was carved except for the identifying heads. They were lengths of the naturally twisted branches, artfully chosen as to shape, each shape different, each shape significant of the character of the piece. They were large. Only looking at them, Lassiter knew that they would be sensually comfortable to the hand.

Two of the pieces were new. They had not been handled enough to glow with the warmth of the others. Both were kings. On the Don's side a spray of twigs grew from the top of the figure. On Lassiter's side a hangman's noose in gold wire was knotted around the neck. Lassiter smiled. The one would represent Elkhorn, the other himself.

He looked toward the work table, back at the Don. He surprised an incongrous pleading in the little eyes, a need to be praised. Lassiter accommodated him.

"An artist made these. A man with as many interests as you have, when do you find the time?"

Miguel looked satisfied, sounded oddly defensive. "Work with the hands. It helps me think. But who on the border plays?"

Lassiter said nothing. So Miguel, at the center of his web, was lonely. It was something else to know about the Don.

The fat man leaned forward. An eagerness showed. "You do, Lassiter. Blood told me so. He told me more, that he didn't intend telling. You are an avenger. You have stolen much from his company. What do you do with all the money?"

"I find uses for it."

The huge head nodded. "Not for yourself, I think. A Robin Hood, perhaps?"

"My business."

"Your business indeed. It's nothing to me. What is interesting is that you laugh at Senor Hume's large network of bloodhound police. Now. We could help each other, I think. Work with me. I can tell you of situations, you can exploit them to advantage. Give me a small percentage of what you collect. I will give you protection. Not only in Orillo. Anywhere. You could be very close to me, Lassiter."

"Sorry."

"You are certain? It could be important to you."

"I work alone."

The fat man swelled with a heavy sigh. "So. I lose you. Perhaps I was too blunt. With a good chess player I should know better, and I suspect you are good." He picked up the Elkhorn figure, caressed it. "You want this man.

He is mine. Let me see if you can win him."

Lassiter put a finger of the king that wore the noose. "And if I lose, I lose a lot?"

The red lips turned back in a thick smile. "You should be encouraged to play your best. Call the coin for first move." He flipped a dollar over the table.

"Heads."

"Tails." The fat man read the face of the coin.

His opening was conventional, king-pawn to king-four. Lassiter countered. It was the king-bishop gambit. The early plays were as stylized, as rigid as ballet. The players felt each other out, probing for weaknessess, judging strengths. Later, Lassiter found a growing warning.

Chess he knew as a game of contra-dictions. The Chinese who developed it, if they did, had had their subtle laugh at government. They made the queen, a woman, the strongest piece on the board. The king they made the weakest. He cannot be taken, yet he is nearly helpless. The whole point of the play is to protect him. When the protection is pierced, when the king is brought to bay, his side has lost the game.

Now Lassiter found another contradiction. Miguel was skilled, too skilled for comfort. It would take luck added to skill to beat him. Now the suggestion came that the Don was not trying to win. There were tiny mistakes. Not obvious. Not many. But mistakes.

Lassiter looked for traps. The afternoon went into night. A servant brought lamps. Lassiter too began to make mistakes. He intended them.

The Don played more slowly, watching Lassiter with new attention. Abruptly he swept the pieces to the center of the board.

"You can play better. You're not trying."

"Neither are you." Lassiter hid faint amusement.

The Don glowered. "You did not win Elkhorn."

"I didn't lose him either. And you still have my thousand dollars in gold."

Miguel sounded peevish. "You knew I was playing to lose."

"Yes."

"Do you know why?"

"Trying to give me Elkhorn without my knowing you were doing it."

The Don shook his head sadly. "Such a smart one you are. I wish you would work with me. We could be good friends."

Lassiter laughed outright. "I've got enough enemies."

The fat shoulders raised and dropped. "So be it. Elkhorn is in Sonora, at Nacozari. Where is my other thousand?"

"You don't get that until I have him."

"He has a lot of friends around him. What if you can't take him?"

"Then you don't get the money."

"I'd be sorry not to have it if you

do take him." There was warning in the tone. Then the fat man chuckled suddenly. "Vaya con Dios, Lassiter."

"Thanks." Lassiter meant it. Any man venturing into the Sierra Madres would need all the help he could get.

7

SIDNEY BLOOD, tilted back in the web seated chair on the hotel porch, watched Lassiter walk brazenly down the street to Don Miguel's house. He knew the man had been summoned, knew what he would be told. It rankled deep in Blood. He too had been summoned and given the Don's decision. The fat man had it all figured out. He had said,

"Senor Blood, you will have to be patient, wait for your chance at Lassiter. I have a use for him first."

He had the enormous arrogance to explain in detail. Lassiter would be told that Elkhorn was in Nacozari, surrounded by friends. He would go there. If he managed to take Elkhorn, he owned the Don a thousand dollars. After that was paid, if the Don still could not bring him into his own organization, Lassiter would be put within reach of Blood. If Lassiter were killed trying to take Elkhorn, then the Don would collect the five thousand dollar reward. He got that either way. It was Lassiter's measly thousand that he wanted as a windfall.

Blood had sat stewing about it. Professionally he would win. Lassiter would be done with. But it was not enough for Blood. Lassiter was his. His nemesis. The one enemy of the company, the one job he had been given that he had not finished. He needed to take Lassiter with his own hands.

It was torture to watch the man walk down that street, within such easy range, and not dare to lift a finger against him. Only one hundred and fifty feet away, and tonight or tomorrow the space would stretch to miles. Lassiter would be riding deep, deeper into the inaccessible reaches of Mexico.

But need that be so? Blood sat up, stung by an idea.

He watched the iron grille close behind his man, jolted the chair down, got up and crossed the plaza to the alley, to the Dean woman's crib. He knocked, waited for her call, took off his hat as he went in, smiled with careful courtesy.

"Don't be frightened, Debbie. I'm here to help you, not to hurt."

Her expression did not change from its hopelessness. She had heard that kind of talk before. She knew not to believe it.

The blond man's voice was gentle, kindly. "How is your daughter these days, Debbie?"

Her eyes changed then, filled with familiar fright. "What daughter?"

"Loli. Don't you remember? The last I heard, she was with Elkhorn in Nacozari. Isn't she still there?"

The woman dropped into the chair, looked up. Blood came forward, sat down on the edge of the bed, reached to take her hand. She shrank back, but he seemed not to notice. He was still smiling.

"I've heard it said that you'd like to get her away from him, that he uses her as a threat to keep you in line. Is that true?"

He could hardly hear her words. "Oh, Jesus." He patted her hand.

"I told you I wanted to help. Here's what I will do. If you will deliver a message for me I promise that I'll get Loli and see you both safely to San Francisco. You'll both be out of Elkhorn's and Miguel's hands. Will you?"

Hope sparked, then was put down. The woman had to moisten her mouth before she could speak.

"What message? Who to?"

Blood showed his pleasure. "To Lassiter. Yes, as a law officer I want him, but also, he is a fellow American. I know that he is going to be sent into an ambush in Mexico. I want to warn him." His tone took on the timbre of truth. Not faked. "I don't want him murdered by that gang down there. I want to take him myself, lawfully, take him back to a lawful court."

The woman showed that she saw little choice. He said,

"Loli?"

"What kind of ambush?"

"Don Miguel is telling him where Elkhorn is. You know Lassiter will go. There are two roads from here south to Nacozari, and Miguel will have an ambush on both of them. Whichever way he goes, he'll be jumped. Tell him to go over to El Paso, to Juarez, but down to Chihuahua City, then turn back across the mountains and into Nacozari from the south. That's all."

She was silent. She looked puzzled, going over the message in her mind. Miguel might indeed set up the ambushes, protecting Elkhorn. And the Wells Fargo man wanted Lassiter north of the border, where he could be taken. That was plain enough. If she carried the message she would warn him of one danger, put him in another. And Lassiter had said he would take her away.

Blood watched her face. Then he said softly,

"Loli?"

Debbie Dean dropped her head into her hands, nodding against them, whispered into them.

"Oh God . . . "

8

THE plaza held the heat stored up through the day. The black air seemed to be compressed under the soggy clouds that had moved in overhead, sultry with the threat of summer rain. Few lights showed on either side of the street. They were dwarfed by occasional sheets of lightning.

One flash burst as Lassiter turned in at the Casa. It blinded him, pulsed behind his eyes. There was no sound from the room behind the lobby desk, where the woman who ran the place usually entertained a lover, no sound in the building.

He felt his way, climbed the stairs. The second floor felt darker than the first. He followed the wall to his door, opened it quietly, half expecting Blood to be there.

At once he sensed there was someone. He held his breath, listening. He heard the faint breathing of the intruder. He placed the sound as close to the bed, took three quick steps. His outstretched left hand found hair, his right a slender throat. He held a woman.

Her gasp, her cry, "You're scalping me," told him who it was. He swung her around, hauled her on a tour of the room. Blood was not there. He let her go, felt for a match. Debbie guessed it, put her hand on his arm.

"No light."

"All right. What are you doing here?"

"I heard from Elkhorn. He's in Nacozari."

"I know."

"Do you know this? Sam Stewart came up from there today. He said Elkhorn and Don Miguel are setting up traps for you somewhere on each road. You can't go directly south, by either Nogales or Agua Prieta."

He wished he could see her face,

read her eyes. He had only her voice to judge by.

"I'm going to Nacozari."

"All right, all right. But there's another way. You can go to El Paso, to Juarez, then south to Chihuahua City, cross the mountains and come back north to Nacozari."

"The old Camino Real?"

"What does that mean?"

He was rigid. Against her warning he struck a match, lighted the lamp. When he turned she was sitting on the floor, huddled out of view from the windows. He squatted in front of her, his lips pulled back.

"It means you're lying. If you knew about that road across the mountains you'd know its name. It's a famous name. You don't learn, do you?"

"Learn what?"

"You set me up for Elkhorn once. You're trying to set me up again."

"I'm telling you the truth."

"You don't know how." Wind blasted through the room. Lightning filled it.

The clouds broke and poured water on Orillo. It was loud in the street, on the roof. "I'll tell you the truth. Miguel has sold me out to Blood. They sent you to con me into riding north, across the border. That's where your ambush is. Blood waiting for me over there." He laughed. "He'll have a long, wet wait. I'm riding south."

"No. No."

Her voice held panic. Too much panic. She knew something else, something she had not told. He caught her hair again, twisted it, dragged her to the window, then pulled viciously. She went halfway through the window and he held her this way by her hair.

"Talk! Or I yank you out the window."

He got the story. Her daughter, thirteen years old, held by Elkhorn, used by him to insure her obedience. Blood's promise to get both of them to San Francisco. Blood's message for Lassiter. Blood's warning her not to let Lassiter know the message was from him.

He blew out the lamp, went to the front window, crouched there, waiting for lightning. When it came the glare lighted the plaza in grotesque brilliance. Sidney Blood stood under the gallery roof of the hotel. There was a saddled horse back in the passage between the hotel and the building next. They were waiting for him to ride north. Debbie had poured out the truth as far as she knew it, but if he rode south he had no assurance that Blood and the Don were not pulling this together, that the trails were not ambushed. Behind him Debbie continued to cry.

She raised her face, parted her hair to look through it. "What are you going to do?"

"Go to Nacozari."

"Take me with you. Help me get Loli."

"No."

She scrambled up, pulling her dress open, thrusting her bare body against him. It was her only weapon. This time it failed her.

He pushed her out of the room, pushed her to the rear stairs, let her go and waited while she ran down them and through the alley door.

Then he went back for his gear.

9

HIS last look out of the front window gave him another brief, sharp picture of the American Hotel. Blood was no longer on the porch. The horse was no longer visible. That would mean that Blood had seen the lamp lighted, seen it extinguished and judged that Lassiter would now make his break.

Blood would, Lassiter thought, now cross the plaza, post himself where he could see the alley and the door of the stable behind the Casa del Orillo, and at the same time see the plaza.

In order to ride north, Lassiter had the choices of circling around the town or riding directly across the plaza. Either way, Blood would see him leave the stable. Blood would be right behind him.

He picked up his gear, saddle and

bedroll, and went down the stairs. He turned through the door into the kitchen, crossed that and went into the corral behind it. The rain struck at him. He lowered his head against it, felt the wind whip at his poncho.

There was no light in the stable. He worked by feel, throwing the saddle on his horse, tying on the roll, quieting the animal. The storm made it nervous. Lightning showed him the rectangle of the alley door, coming in more frequent flashes now. He turned and led the horse into the corral, across it and into the kitchen. On the earth floor its hoofs made little sound. He walked it through the hallway door and down the hall to the street entrance. He propped open the front door, led the horse onto the dark colonnade outside. In the drive of the rain he could hear nothing. He could see nothing, not the length of his arm.

If he was right, Blood would be standing under the colonnade just across the alley. Not forty feet away.

He felt for the stirrup, lifted his foot and fitted it, and as he put his weight up the plaza blazed with light. He threw his leg across the saddle, raked both spurs deep in the horse's flanks. He had one glimpse of Blood, his head coming around as he caught the movement, his hand going down to the gun on his hip. Then his animal had leaped through the arch into the deep mud of the plaza, was bolting across it, through blackness.

The light was gone, leaving all eyes blinded. But the heavy splash of the horse's feet rose over the drum of falling water.

Behind him Blood's gun exploded. In Orillo. Whether in the extremity of desperation or as a reflex action Lassiter could not say. Then he was across the plaza, the horse swerving sharply, veering away from the hotel building, veering again to drive into the passage beside it.

Lassiter was on the American side, hearing the splatter of Blood's horse as it ran through the mud. He could not tell how close Blood was, how fast his reaction had been in mounting. Not until he was clearing the rear of the buildings and his noise stopped echoing off the walls. Then he heard Blood enter the passage.

He put his start at a short sixty feet. In daylight Blood could knock him out of the saddle with a shot. If a bolt of lightning struck now and held long enough he would be easy to hit.

The light came, but it was short. It would blind Blood as it blinded him, the image of what he saw shattered immediately by the sudden return of blackness.

Blood was shooting now, repeated shots searching the trail for him.

Ahead the ground rolled. There was only the single trail. In daylight he would have cut aside, cut through the mounds. He did not dare risk it now. He had to keep to the trail, trust the horse to find solid footing. Trust that lightning would not expose him too often.

The rain beat at him, soaked him, flooded his eyes. If he could see nothing through the dark, he could see less through the stinging water.

It was going to be a race. Whichever horse was the better would win it. Lassiter's was a good horse, a race horse that he'd won in a poker game. He laid his head down along the withers and spurred the animal. He drove for the Little Dragoons. The horse did not like the going. He forced it.

Two miles north of town he felt the lift of the first ridges. The curtain of rain was lighter, the storm front passing. The blackness was less intense. If it kept on this way there should be a place where he could turn off, wait for Blood, shoot his horse from under him.

He would not shoot the man. He knew Blood, understood the man's thought processes, could outguess him.

And Blood worked alone. He wanted to take Lassiter alone.

If he killed Blood the whole resources of the Wells Fargo machine would be turned out on his trail, not a single man with whom he was familiar. Nobody knew how many special agents they had, how many informers were on their payroll, selling information to the San Francisco office.

The horse lunged, plunging up as the grade steepened. A side canyon opened, more felt than seen. Lassiter swung the animal into the mouth and pulled it up. It was glad to stop. Blood had not appeared within five minutes. Lassiter had no illusion that the man had quit. Something had held him up.

The rain slacked further. Over it he heard a growing sound. A greater threat than the man behind him. The grinding roar of flash flood water boiling down the draw.

He dropped out of the saddle, scrambled up the canyon side, slipping in the greasy ground, dragging the frightened horse after him. He was still climbing when the crest of the raging wall swept below him, threw rocks, bushes, animals into the air around him.

He stopped, worked at getting his breath, hearing the flood growl toward the main trail, wondering if Sidney Blood was caught in its path.

When it was gone, silence shut down. It took him minutes to realize that the rain had stopped. The clouds were racing overhead, thinning, the sky lightening.

He did not return to the road. He went on across the rising hills, letting the horse pick its way. After midnight he made a cold camp, a wet one. He did not dare risk a fire. He pulled the horse down on its side and lay down with it, curling his body against the warm hide.

In the morning his clothes were still soggy. The early sun lifted steam from the horse and man alike. He had ridden without food, without coffee. Water was not a problem at the moment. Every small gully had its rushing stream filled with silt brought down from the higher mountains, the run-off of the cloudburst. That would pass. In twenty-four hours the canyon bottoms would again be powder dry.

He did not ride for Wilcox. If Blood had survived the flash flood he would head straight for the town. Lassiter turned his horse eastward, through the jumbled breaks of the tortured mountains, toward a small mine that sat alone in a barren box canyon.

Three days later he came into El Paso. It was after midnight, but the border capital was noisily awake. He avoided the street, bringing his horse along the alley and through the rear door of the livery. The barn man was not glad to see him. Still, they had done business before and would again.

"Blood was in town, asking about you."

"When?"

"Yesterday."

"Still here?"

"He rode out this morning, heading south. At least that's what he said."

Lassiter considered. Blood was worse than a cat for extra lives. The flood had not caught him.

"I need food and a fresh horse."

He watched the man leave the livery, transferred gold from his money belt to his pocket, led the horse into a box stall, pulled off the saddle and blanket. Without rubbing it down he turned it into the rear corral, then he lay down on the matted hay and slept.

An hour later the barn man waked him. He had a grub sack of beans, coffee, dried meat, flour. Lassiter paid him, told him to care for his horse, saddled and mounted the fresh animal. Then he rode without hurry toward the river and put the horse across the shallow water.

Juarez was lively. He detoured through its twisting streets, keeping out of the lighted areas, passed the last of the straggling shanties and took the road south, toward Chihuahua City.

He did not know where Sidney Blood was, and he didn't like it. He didn't want to have to kill the agent. He had hoped Blood would stay north of the line. He had no legal business in Mexico.

The road was good, the main highway north and south, east of the mountains. One of the few serviceable roads in northern Mexico.

He rode at night, pulling off into the bordering hills and resting through the days, and it took him four nights to reach Chihuahua. He had traveled a thousand miles and he was farther from Nacozari than he had been in Orillo.

Chihuahua was a city. Lassiter doubted that even the Mexican government knew how large it was, but he put his guess at over ten thousand people living in the rabbit warren of hovels huddled around the gleaming white Federal Palace and the plaza.

The Palace was like any other in that country. Thick walled, low, faced with an arched colonnade. What set it apart from the others was its decoration. Hundred of Apache scalps hung along the colonnade, from the windows. Grinning Apache heads stuck on top of long poles marched around the border of the plaza. Grisly reminders of the unheaval in Central Mexico when the Apaches had swooped down out of the mountains, killed the men and carried off the women and children to slavery.

The reaction had been the Protecto de Guerra, passed by the Chihuahua government in eighteen thirty-seven. It was a bounty act, offering a hundred dollars American for the scalp of an Apache warrior, fifty for a woman. A child was worth twenty-five.

It was a panic law, and it brought results. American outlaws, trappers, buffalo hunters gravitated to the Sierra Madres to take advantage of the market. Lassiter knew some of the men who had gone south. There were a lot of them down here. And in numbers they were formidable. Elkhorn belonged to that fraternity.

Lassiter rode below the heads, past the Palace. Two blocks beyond he got down, tied the horse and went into the dark of a small cantina.

It was a low room with earth floor, blackened beams, a mean bar against one wall. Half a dozen customers sat at the two tables pulled together in the center of the room, laughing at the two girls with them. The girls were half naked, entertaining the men in a competition of making one breast dance independently of the other. The laughter stopped when Lassiter came through the door. The attention turned on him, resentful and suspicious. A wall went up. Behind it were memories of experiences with Americans.

Lassiter walked across the floor that was gummy in spots with old spilled liquor. He came against the bar in front of the woman behind it, a square blocky figure with a flat Indian face.

"Bennie Huie."

His voice was low, but behind him chairs grated on the earth, two men got up from the table, settled the long knives in their belts, came at him from two sides. Their bare feet made little sound.

Lassiter did not seem to see. He watched the woman. She had not answered. Her eyes were black, flat, sliding past him to the men. They were out of his sight. There was no mirror here.

"Tell Bennie it's Lassiter."

Her face did not change and she might have been stone deaf. The two men stopped behind Lassiter, boxing him in, their hands on the hilts of the knives. The room waited. Death waited impatiently in the room.

The woman stepped back and padded down the bar to the arch at the end, pushed aside a green curtain there, put her head through it. The silence ran on, heavy. Then the head appeared again, jerked an invitation.

"Pasar."

The tension of the room broke on the word. Like breaking glass. The men went back to the table. Lassiter went through the curtain to the rear room.

Cell was a closer description. There was no window, light came from a wick floating in a dish of oil on a table, the table was cluttered with papers. A redheaded man sat at the table, a quill pen in his hand poised above a paper, his green eyes on the curtain. Lassiter dropped the curtain behind him, shutting the hostility outside.

Bennie Huie did not stand up in greeting. He had no legs to stand on. The stumps, padded in black leather, stuck out foolishly from the chair seat. The legs were back in the caved mine that Lassiter had pulled him out of six years before. He looked at Lassiter without surprise or curiosity.

"I thought I smelled you in the neighborhood. Welcome back."

"That's good to hear." Lassiter hooked a thumb over his shoulder. "I didn't hear it out there. They'd rather have knifed me."

"We've had some trouble with Streeter's gang. The boys are edgy." The green eyes glinted. "You wouldn't even have got here if I hadn't passed a word around."

Lassiter nodded, his smile brief.

Huie said, "A man was in Chihuahua three days ago. Asking for you. He was offering five hundred dollars."

"Sidney Blood."

"Sidney Blood."

"What did you tell him?"

"I didn't see him. He didn't know I was here."

"He still around?"

"He rented mules, hired a mozo. They took the road to Minaca."

Lassiter nodded again. The road to Nacozari started at Minaca. Elkhorn was in Nacozari. Blood knew that Lassiter would go there. The thing was simplicity itself.

"I need mules too."

"To go to Minaca?"

"Yes."

Huie watched him gravely. "You want some advice?"

"No."

"You'll get it anyway, because I owe you. Don't go. There's nothing worth a centavo in that country except lost mines."

"Maybe I like lost mines."

Huie sat back in his chair and closed his eyes, tickling his temple with the feathered quill.

"The trail to Sonora climbs over the roughest hills on the continent. It drops down gorges where you reach out and touch both walls at once. It used to carry the heaviest traffic in the country, supplies for the Spanish mines going in, one burro train biting at the tail of another. Silver and gold for the King of Spain going out like a river. Then the Indians attacked and the industry went to hell. There's nothing left of the mines, ranches, towns, except ruin.

You can ride six days and not see another man. But the Indians are still in there, and they don't like Americans any better than they like Mexicans. The bounty hunters are there too. They don't care how long or what color a scalp is. They always see you before you see them."

"Where can I buy mules?"

The green eyes opened. The shoulders lifted.

"Vaya con Dios."

It sounded like an echo. The last time he had heard the phrase, Don Miguel had used it. In neither case was it a blessing. Both times it had sounded like a rattler's warning.

10

SIDNEY BLOOD rode his mule into Nacozari at noon. His mozo, trotting tirelessly behind the loaded pack burro, took both animals and the three went thankfully toward the mud walled corral. They had been ten days on the trail from Chihuahua. Blood had lost twenty pounds. He was relieved to be in even this debatable civilization again.

Nacozari sat on the site of a very old town, probably an Indian settlement long before the Spanish conquistadores overran it in their northward push, lusting after gold. In 1646 it was destroyed in an uprising of the Indian peon slaves. When it was rebuilt it was harassed by Yaquis. Apache raids swept through it in bloody slaughter and kidnapping forays. Treachery and terror and time it had survived.

Now it enjoyed a certain peace. That group of scalp hunters who headquartered here, rallying around Casimero Streeter, were master at beating off Indian raids. For that service the Mexican officials tolerated them and their fringe, the smugglers, prospectors, opportunists.

Blood had been here before, but then he had come south from Nogales, not across the killing Sierra Madre trail. His muscles ached from the trip. He walked stiffly across the plaza, the only moving being. It was siesta. The natives slept. Even the rawhide race that prowled the mountains took their ease in the middle of the day.

Blood was admitted to the Streeter hacienda by the armed guard who kept the gate. He entered a patio let go to ruin but paved with old inlaid tiles that had been taken from the remains of an early mission church.

Streeter was not a big man, but there was power enough in his body to kill with bare hands. He had done it more than once. He had surfaced in California in time to join Fremont in the Bear State revolt, had killed an army officer and fled to New Mexico.

There, he joined the Apaches, rode with them, raided with them, earned the nickname, White Apache. The White Apache he had been ever since, even after he turned against the tribe to hunt its scalps with the same enthusiasm that he had earlier hunted down white settlers. It was a name that spread terror throughout the Sierra Madres.

He sat in his patio, his shirt off, hairy chest bared to the hot sun, his skin leathered and as tanned as a genuine Apache.

Elkhorn sat across the table. They were drinking pulque from painted gourds, playing cards. Half a dozen of Streeter's men drowsed in the shade, tired and trail worn, just returned from the headwater of the Yaqui River, the ten scalps they had taken still tied at their belts.

Blood did not like the smell in the

patio. He stopped just inside the grilled gate, watching the men, watching for reaction.

One, sprawled under a mesquite tree, rolled to his knees, his hand slapping at his gun, his voice sharp.

"Wells Fargo."

Blood grinned, called. "I'm not after you, Crouse. This is out of my territory."

Crouse did not move. His hand stayed on the gun. Streeter's laugh broke the moment.

"Clear out of here, Crouse, vamoose. The rest of you too."

Crouse got up slowly, resentful, waited while the others straggled to their feet, then they filed past Blood. Their eyes raked him. He was their natural enemy. They wanted him. But they did not go against Streeter.

Blood stayed quiet, watchful, until the gate closed on the last of them. Then he walked to the table, dropped to the chair between Streeter and Elkhorn and helped himself to a drink from the pulque gourd. His face twisted at the sour milk taste.

"Can't you afford decent liquor?"

Streeter's eyes moved about with an animal's hungry restlessness. Elkhorn was nervous, his fingers crimping the cards in his hand. Both Blood's hands were on the table. He cocked the right thumb and forefinger at the man.

"You remember me, Elkhorn, don't you?"

The nervous tongue ran around gray lips. The head nodded, uncertain.

Blood sat back lazily, his tone lazy. "That was a sloppy job you pulled in Harmony. You didn't get a dime. I wonder why?"

Elkhorn only looked at him.

The lazy tone went on. "Don Miguel is tired of you. He sold you out to Lassiter."

"Lassiter . . . he's dead." Elkhorn's eyes jumped. He wanted to recall the words.

Blood's grin was thin. He let the man sweat. Then, holding the grin, his lips straight, he said quietly, "He's a hard man to hold in jail. If I'd known about the holdup in time I could have warned Sheriff Frost to ball and chain him. The first I knew was the reward notices that he'd broken free. By the time I got to Harmony he was back in Orillo. Looking for you."

Elkhorn's throat was dry. "Where is he now?"

The grin stayed. "On his way here. I told you the fat man sold you out. For two thousand dollars."

Streeter bent across the table, slapped it. "You're talking crazy."

Blood's grin turned on him. "When did I lie to you?"

They looked at each other. The scalp hunter quit first.

"I thought he was smarter. If its true, it's the end of the fat man, end of Orillo."

"No. Elkhorn isn't in Orillo."

Elkhorn exploded. "Don't listen to him. He's lying."

Streeter laughed at him, enjoying

watching Elkhorn squirm. "Miguel sent you down here on the quiet. How did Blood know where to find you?" He winked at Blood.

They waited. Elkhorn was slow witted. It took him time. Finally he pulled his head down between his shoulders.

"Damn him."

Sidney Blood did not like puzzles, and he was puzzled. He had broken Elkhorn open. Now his tone turned conversational.

"Tell me about Harmony."

Elkhorn glowered and stayed silent. Streeter lifted a single finger, pointed it like a gun.

"Yes. Tell us."

Elkhorn's eyes pleaded with him. Streeter kept pointing. Blood prodded.

"You didn't get money from that bank. Not one penny."

Elkhorn caved. "We weren't supposed to. I guess if the bastard sold me out I don't need to keep quiet. The fat man set up the kill with Frost, the sheriff.

The banker was his brother. He wanted the bank and his brother's wife."

Streeter sounded disbelieving. "But you didn't get the money? Where's the payoff?"

"Frost was afraid we'd clean out the bank. I don't know what Miguel got, he gave me a thousand to split with the boys."

Blood said, "With Lassiter too?"

"Hell no."

"Why did you pick him for the fall guy?"

"I didn't. The fat man did. Lassiter was new in Orillo, but he had a record, a reputation. Any jury would vote that he'd rob a bank, shoot his way out."

"He told me he didn't shoot."

Elkhorn hesitated, looked at the hard eyes pushing him. He did not dare to lie here.

"It was rigged for him not to have a gun in his hand. We sent him in through the rear. I took two men in the front and shot the banker. Naturally, Lassiter ducked back outside, and the deputies the sheriff had planted on the roof dropped on him."

Blood chuckled in spite of himself. It was a rare pleasure to hear that Lassiter had been deliberately trapped. Then bleakness settled on him again. Not because Elkhorn admitted to the hired murder. Not for the perfidy of a sheriff. Not for a woman who might be an innocent victim. But because Lassiter had again made a laughing stock of the law. A wave of futility crested in him.

Elkhorn sat silent, his mind looking back at the man who was coming for him. Abruptly he shoved back his chair, got to his feet. Streeter looked up, displeased to be startled.

"Where do you think you're going?"

Elkhorn's answer was prompt. "I'm clearing out. Heading south. For Hermosillo, Guaymas, catch a boat for South America."

"Not far enough." Blood's voice rasped over the file of bitterness. "No place is far enough. You've got a crocodile on your tail for the rest of your life."

Streeter's laugh was shrill, chill because it was incongruous. "Hey, that's good. I read about that crocodile when I was a kid." Sudden insight narrowed his eyes. "Same way you're on his tail, isn't 'it?"

Elkhorn cursed. "What do you expect me to do, sit here like a crippled duck, wait to get killed?"

Blood drew a deep breath, gave in to the futility, gave up his long, lone trailing.

"You might kill him instead."

Streeter heard the tone. He heaved to his feet, walked to the olla hanging in the shade, had a drink of water. He brought half a gourd full back, filled it with pulque and swallowed it.

"Where is he now?"

"I don't know."

"What the hell . . .?"

"I don't know. There was a hell of a storm in Orillo. He rode out in it and I lost him. He was headed north, but he could have circled back down through Nogales. I came down by Juarez. No sign of him there, none on the road, none in Chihuahua. None across the Sierras."

"Maybe he's not coming." Elkhorn was hopeful.

"He's coming. Should have been here by now." Blood flushed, frustration crowded him. "Damn it, where is he?"

Streeter grinned, liking to see Wells Fargo off balance. "Probably pulled out of the road, let you go by him. Probably moseying along enjoying the scenery."

Blood's flush deepened. He had been so intent on his chase that he hadn't thought of that. But it was what Lassiter would do. In the pattern. The unexpected.

He could not hide the new excitement. "So much the better. He can be caught in the mountains."

Streeter dropped into his chair. Lazy now. "Easy enough east of the Sonora border, there's only one trail. If he's crossed the ridge he's got a choice of several trails. Might be on any one of them. Where to find him depends on how far behind you he is."

Blood's impatience made him restless in the chair. "Get your men into the hills. Cover every trail from Chihuahua. If they can find an Apache they can find him."

Streeter brought out his knife, cleaned the nails of one hand, let Blood sweat. "How much?"

"He's after a friend of yours. You don't want him here."

"I don't have friends. I'm a business man." Streeter raised his eyes, speculative, to Blood's uncovered head. "That's a pretty crop of yellow hair you're wearing."

Blood jarred. Streeter lunged the knife forward, shook its point.

"The Mexicans won't pay one nickel for Lassiter's scalp. What will you pay?"

Lassiter on the ground. A man

kneeling, running a blade around the crown of his hair. The picture came up sharp.

"Five hundred."

Streeter's lip curled. "For a minute I thought you wanted him."

Blood knew he was baited, but he had come too far into the blaze of hope. Its heat seared him. Burned his reason. Into the hands of James Hume, head of Wells Fargo police, he must deliver Lassiter's scalp. He would suffocate unless he got that scalp.

"Five hundred for you. Five hundred for the man who brings me that hair."

11

FROM Chihuahua the treasure road ran west, lifting into the moist, forested mountains, crossed the Continental Divide and dropped down the arid, barren western slopes to the village of Minaca. The Camino Real. The Silver Road. Over it the Spaniard had hauled his burro trains loaded with the wealth torn out of the brutal hills of the mining district. Nameless, the road was older than Mexico itself, used by the Indians before the memory of history. It was the only way across the great spine of the land. Long use had made it not a bad road.

Westward from Minaca, like the roots of a tree, individual trails made tendrils through the sea of mountains, inched toward the headwaters of the Yaqui and its sister, south-flowing rivers, sought out those isolated pockets where the rich ores had been discovered. Westward of Minaco the land was cruel by nature, primitive as it had been when the mountains lifted, barely pricked by man's minuscule scratching at it.

Minaca had been the headquarters, the staging point for shipping. Into it had flowed the fabulous wealth destined for Spain.

That traffic was all gone now. The locations of the mines were lost during the Indian rebellion, unknown to the white men. The people of Minaca were descendants of the Indian slaves with whom the priests had worked the mines. The people knew where the old workings were. They would not tell. Gold and silver had brought only misery to their forebears. They wanted no mining to destroy them again. Occasional sun blackened Americans came through with maps and ancient charts that had been carried away by the Jesuits when the slaves had destroyed the mines, burned the churches, driven out the priests. They were met with the blank face of noncomprehension.

The village nestled under the shadow of the Cerro Minaca, the mountain that lifts startling, abrupt, from the high plain. Lassiter came over the Camino Real, dropped into Minaca and stopped his mules in front of the dissolving mud hut that passed for the inn. He bent his head to go through the low door. After a minute he made out the shape of the innkeeper.

The man was squat, square, swarthy, mustachioed. A black cheroot hung, pasted to his lower lip. Its smoke rose straight, not disturbed by movement of the burning end. The black eyes stared, hostile, stoic.

Lassiter nodded. "I want Don Raphael. Huie said he's here."

The dark eyes blinked, slow as an owl's. "I do not know either name, Senor."

He was lying. Both of them knew it. Before the blind, deaf, stubborn silence of these people a traveller was helpless. No bribe, no threat would bring reaction. Lassiter did not try.

"So be it." He turned aside, into the gloom of the saloon, asked for pulque, sat down at the little corner table and gave his attention to the bottle.

From the other room came querulous Spanish voices, too low to be understood. It could be an argument. He caught the word 'explorador,' prospector, then another indistinguishable rattle. After that he sat for an hour in silence. At least the thick walls, the deep roof, kept out the sun.

The whisper of bare feet on the earth floor made him look toward the door. A mozo was there, wide sombrero, serape, a long shirt, no pants, beckoning. There was more arrogant command than servility in the gesture.

Lassiter rang a coin on the table and followed. There was no one in sight outside. The thick dust of the street muffled their steps. At the end of the street squatted the white stucco church crowned with the small, placid bell tower. Behind, in its shade, the mozo stopped at a door, pointed to it, turned and trotted away.

Inside was a single room. The only furniture was a pile of bright blankets on the floor, where a man sat. His head was small, round, Indian. His eyes were a surprise, keen, questioning. He wore the shapeless white shirt and cotton breeches of a peon, but something in his face, a trace of finer chiseling, marked him apart. He saw all there was to see of Lassiter before he said.

"Why does Huie send you to me?"

Lassiter had Huie's note in his hand. He held it out, walking forward. Don Raphael accepted it in long, graceful fingers, read it, returned it. His hand made a gentle flourish.

"My house is yours."

Lassiter was relieved. Huie's agents wandered through the hills picking up the small amounts of gold brought in by the Indians when they wanted cash. Most of the gold buyers cheated the sellers as a matter of course. Huie did not, and was trusted. But you never knew.

"A blond man rode through here. Did he ask for me?"

Don Raphael was rising in belated hospitality. "He asked."

"What was he told?"

The Don's eyebrows climbed. "In Minaca? Nothing is told here, Senor."

Lassiter did not hide his small smile. "How far ahead is he?"

"Two days. He traded two burros for two fresh ones."

"I need to do the same. I need something else. A man I can trust, who can ride while I walk."

The questioning eyes studied him. Lassiter's smile widened.

"The blond man will buy others to waylay me on the trail. I need a disguise. I will be the mozo, my guide will ride ahead."

Was it laughter behind the quiet face? It surely was not reluctance. The man flicked a finger at Huie's note.

"Who wants a man to trust, trusts

himself. I am pleased to repay many favors."

They took the trail at daylight, Don Raphael riding a fine Spanish mule, leading a pack burro carrying supplies. Lassiter trotted humbly behind the animals. Raphael had trimmed his hair round, in the Indian fashion, crowned it with a conical straw hat, given him a cotton shirt and baggy pants. His skin had been stained with a mix of cochineal and earth pigment rubbed in deep. The effect was to give him the red tone that underlay the bronze of the native. Huaraches of woven leather strips were a concession on which Raphael insisted. The white man could not run so far in bare feet. The shoes would be accepted if an inspection came.

The trail Don Raphael chose was little used. It led up canyons, across the rocky, reaching fingers of rising mountains. It crossed high, timbered mesas, dropped a mile into the canyon of the Mayo. From above the floor it looked down on the ruins of old ranches, orange trees still bearing among the prickly trunks of cotton trees slowly strangling them. They bottomed out, crossed the river, climbed again, into the red-hued madrones festooned in silkworm cocoons.

In three hundred miles there was not a house with a window. The widely scattered Indians crouched in smoke filled caves or pole structures with mud walls and matted roofs. The land gave up nothing willingly, yet the stark shapes under the brilliant blue spread of sky rose to grandeur, the earth color held the warmth of a woman's body. It was a land that challenged, tempted, killed.

Lassiter moved across its vastness one step at a time. Through the early days Raphael turned often, looked back, sure that no white man could make the passage on foot. In time he quit looking. He admired the way the man hid the evening campfires. Squatting beside them he began to talk about the country. Lassiter showed no suspicious interest.

Watching closely, Raphael told the story of the lost Tayopa mine.

"Men have looked for it for many years, but never found it. It was said to be one of the richest."

Lassiter shook his head. "Don't look at me. I've seen men gone crazy chasing dreams like that. The Indians probably know where it is. And they're welcome to it. All I want here is one man. And to avoid another."

The story proved one point to Lassiter. Don Raphael was beginning to trust him.

Progress was slow. On their best day they managed twenty miles. Through the rougher canyons and deeper gorges they were lucky to make ten. There were passages pinched in so close that Raphael climbed down and walked through rather than scrape his knees on the rock walls. Beyond each of these he argued that Lassiter should ride for awhile.

"They may be waiting around the next bend," became the expected answer.

They reached the Sonora line. Not that there was a marker or any change in the rumpled hills. Don Raphael said they were in Sonora, and he knew the country.

Two hours later Raphael swung his mule into an intersecting trail, the first they had passed in a hundred miles. Lassiter turned in without question, but the Don stopped, motioned him forward.

"A little side trip. Something you should see."

"I haven't got time. Kick that mule around and let's go."

"You're too rigid in your purpose, Senor. Like a horse with blinders. If you see only what is straight ahead you miss what comes at you from the angle."

He kicked the mule ahead. Lassiter had the choice of shooting him or following, and killing his guide would not be very smart.

They climbed a V shaped canyon in single file. There wasn't room to go abreast. The ground was so overgrown that Lassiter would not have recognized a trail. With the sun at the zenith the rocks radiated heat, yet there was a downdraft. Its source was a break where the wall receded grudgingly, a side draw carved and polished by water rushing down it at some time past. A waterfall had brightened the place once. There was no moisture now, only the parched breastwork of glossy stone.

Raphael clambered to its top and sat until Lassiter came up. Behind it was a depression that had held a pool. There was not enough dampness in it now to rot the scattered skeletons bleached as ivory. Lassiter counted three human skulls, the assorted bones of several burros. He frowned at Raphael.

"We wasted half an hour to look at this?"

Raphael tossed a stone at a snake stretched in the shade of a blanket caught in a thorn bush, its corner lifting and falling with the breeze. The snake contracted, pointed its tail up, vibrated the thimble of rattles, drew its flat head back over its coils and looked for the enemy that had disturbed it.

"These are men who tried to take gold out of this place. I thought you should see it before I show you the valley."

"I told you I'm not interested in gold."

Raphael raised his shoulders eloquently. He might have said aloud that he did not put his trust in words. He returned to the animals, mounted, put the mule up the slope of the draw.

Lassiter stood at the bottom of the rocks, spread legged, looking up.

"Is this the road to Nacozari or are you playing games?"

Raphael turned in his saddle. He was polite but definite. "Do you want to get there used up and face a man

143

who is fresh? We'll rest in the valley tonight and tomorrow and tomorrow night."

Lassiter stood where he was, five hundred miles from nowhere. The mule with his guide on it, the burro carrying the water, food, his guns, tipped their rumps over the nose of the bowl and went out of sight. After a moment he chose to laugh. Raphael had him cold. He began to climb.

Just before sunset they wound down through a shallow canyon thick with thorn bush. The valley opened beyond it. The slanting rays from the west cast the small world in glittering relief, washed it in bronze.

A flowing stream. Grass. Trees. Incredibly, peaches, quince, pomegranate, oranges.

Don Raphael said, "And the only bananas that grow in Sonora. We'll eat well tonight."

Lassiter's breath came in, filled him. His muscles quivered. He had not known that he was tired. His lips curved.

"You win."

Raphael's smile broke white.

They made camp against the stream. Lassiter caught a glimpse of movement through the trees, saw that a deer was nibbling among the branches, and shot it. They cooked the liver and ate fresh meat for the first time since leaving Minaca. Lassiter slept the night through. Raphael did not wake him for the second watch.

In the morning he made a tour of the valley. Above the camp was the remains of a smelter. An oak tree probably two hundred years old grew up through the rough brick grinding floor. Not far away he found the old mine shaft, picked up a stone and tossed it down the dark hole. It was long seconds before the echo of a splash came up the walls.

He turned back through the trees, the smell of ripening fruit heavy around him. He thought of the arid mountains they had crossed, of the Indians there punching holes in the ground with a sharp stick, planting corn kernel, nursing the growth of a poverty crop.

He smelled coffee before he saw the camp. Raphael was awake, working beside the fire. Lassiter accepted a plate from him.

"Why isn't anyone living in here?"

Raphael looked into the firelight. "It belongs to the Old Ones. The Indos won't stay here after dark."

"You spent the night here."

Raphael winked. "I've got Spanish blood. It makes a difference."

"Why don't you come and work the property?"

"You saw the skeletons. I'm a poor man, but I'm alive."

Through the day Lassiter deliberately relaxed. Normally he caught what rest he could in the brief opportunities that offered. Lately there had been little time. He took off the huaraches, went to the stream, bathed his feet and cared for them. Then he coated them in mud, let it dry into a hard cake, feeling it pull the soreness from them.

Toward evening he was again at the fire, watching Raphael slice more deer liver and put it on to cook. The pungent odor was tempting, lifting into the air.

Sound caught his attention. He looked to the mouth of the valley. Two men were riding in, bearded, roughly dressed, Americans. They could have been prospectors. Except that scalps hung from both saddles.

Their guns were in their hands. Lassiter's were in the pack, Raphael's rifle lay against a rock beyond reach. Lassiter regretted relaxing.

The pair rode to the fire, sitting above them, making no move to dismount. One was near Lassiter's size, the other a red bearded giant. That one eased himself in his saddle.

"Kind of late in the day for you to be hanging around here, ain't it?"

Raphael sat back on his haunches, looking up. There was a dignity about him, drawn from the mountains, from the people from whom he came.

"We will be gone before dark, Senor."

"That so?" The big man nudged an elbow at his companion. "Think we can palm that hair off as Apache?"

Lassiter knew that it was not a joke. Half the scalps on which bounty was collected had not come from Apache heads. Any Indian would do if they could catch him alone. And they were caught. He stayed quiet. The men backed away and climbed down, one at a time, watchful. The big one wrinkled his nose at the cooking meat.

"I'm hungry, Joe. Let's eat first."

He came forward as the other hobbled the horses, then walked to Raphael's rifle, picked it up by the barrel, broke it across the rock. The stock snapped off. The man threw the pieces aside.

After a mule, a rifle was the most important thing a man in the mountains could have. Knowing Raphael now,

Lassiter caught the small tightening at the corner of his eyes, otherwise the Don appeared not to notice the destruction. He merely nodded toward the cooking meat.

"What we have is yours, Senors."

The big one grinned, winked at his fellow. "How'd you guess, cholo?" He came in, pulling a knife from his belt. The knife was already bloody. He speared a piece of liver, blew at it to cool it, and gnawed at it. "Mozo, bring that water over here."

Lassiter went warily, played the part. The redhead dipped the cup in the pail, drank. In a sudden move he flung half the cupful at Lassiter's face. Lassiter stumbled back as he was expected to. Both men laughed at him.

The big one pointed his bright blade. "Come here, you."

Lassiter moved forward again. He hoped his disguise would hold at close quarters. The knife aimed upward at his chest.

"Either of you seen a white man on

the trail, coming from Chihuahua?"

Lassiter moved his head sideways, slowly.

"What are you doing here?"

Raphael said, "Rest . . . " Lassiter's voice cut over him. "We were looking for gold, Senor."

It caught their attention. "Find any?"

"A little."

There was a loosening of muscles, a shifting of intent. The big man lifted to his feet like a snake uncoiling, hitched his thumbs in his belt.

"Let's see what you got."

Raphael, with the blood of slaves in him, with the vow of silence drummed through his childhood ears, reacted by instinct. He answered on reflex.

"No."

The second man jumped, his back-hand raked across Raphael's mouth. Raphael fell into the fire. He scrambled out, dancing, brushing at the hot embers. The scalp hunters hooted. Their attention was away from Lassiter.

His cry was frightened. "I'll get it.

It's in the pack." His run looked like a scared rabbit. He dropped to his knees, scrabbling at the ties, bent over the pack. His back was exposed. They could shoot him now. He counted on surprise.

When he twisted back he held his guns on them. He yelled once. To focus them away from Raphael. On him.

They swung, their hands slapping toward their holsters. Lassiter held his fire. Their kind knew this game. Their first look was toward his hands. They stopped moving, stood frozen. Then thought came. The redhead cursed.

"That's no Indian. That's Lassiter."

Lassiter stood up. "How much am I worth to Blood?"

The smaller man's eyes were hungry on him. He could not stop the hungry words. "Five hundred."

Raphael had not waited, had moved in behind the smaller man, lifted his guns, thrown them away. He stepped against the big redhead, wrapped his arms around to the front, took hold of the butts of the holstered guns. It took his full reach.

The big man was fast. He caught one arm, yanked Raphael off balance, pulled him in front of him, hugged him against his chest. Lassiter could not shoot without hitting Raphael. He did not fire. He jumped, both hands up, came against Raphael, slashed with both barrels, across the Indian's head, raked the redhead's skull.

The giant lurched back, did not go down, got his hands around Raphael's ribs and flung him across, into Lassiter. The reeling, falling body came with enough impact to knock Lassiter off his feet, landed on top of him.

The giant was bearing on him. Lassiter heaved Raphael away, doubled his legs to find his footing. A kicking boot caught the side of his head, arced him back to the ground, damaged him. His guns fell. His hands could not hold them.

The giant reared back, drew in his

gut to pull the knife at his belt, dove at Lassiter. Lassiter had rolled. The man hit the ground where he had been. The knife went hilt deep in the matted grass.

Coming to his knees, Lassiter looked for his guns. One was out of sight. The other five feet away. Five feet too far away. The redhead was on his way. The knife's broad blade pointed at him, held out from the man's middle.

Lassiter swiveled, spinning to his feet. He caught the knife wrist as it thrust past him. He had momentum enough to jar his hip into the thick thigh, to pivot, carry the knife arm over his shoulder, pitch the man over his head.

He was still turning. In the blur that passed his eyes the smaller man was bent, his hand stretched for a gun on the ground. Lassiter came around again, his foot swinging. It clubbed against the man's side. Barefoot, the kick knocked the man over, did not crack the ribs.

Lassiter was yelling at Raphael to get a gun. Raphael lay retching where he had dropped, choking for air. He doubled to his knees, his head on the ground. Lassiter did not see if he made it, the redhead was coming again.

The knife was gone. The big arms were stretched wide, forward, reaching for a bear hug. He was there.

Lassiter stepped inside, drove a fist into the stomach. In the second's hiatus he chopped at the bull neck with the side of his other hand, below the ear. The head snapped sidewise. Lassiter clubbed his knee into the groin.

The constricting arms lost their strength. He hit the neck again. The body slumped away, the convulsed hands dragged Lassiter with him.

A gun exploded. Lassiter rolled free and looked. The smaller scalp hunter jerked against the ground as if he head were staked to it. The front of the head was red. The face was gone. Raphael stood beyond him, the lowered gun in his hand leaking smoke. He lifted the gun again, walked to where the redhead was on his knees, rump in the air, lurching to get his feet under him. He took aim on the bright hair and shot through it.

The sun was gone, the afterglow a brilliant red of silent thunder. Death belonged here. It had lived here for centuries. Raphael still apologized. His eyes were defensive on Lassiter.

"They broke my gun."

Lassiter got up, settled his clothes, kicked through the grass until he found his own guns. He took them back to the pack, tidied it. There would not be other visitors like this tonight. There was an ethic among these men. They did not hunt in each other's territories.

There would be visitors though. Coyotes, cats perhaps, scavengers, drawn to a feast. He brought a horse, tied a rope to the feet of the dead men, dollied it around the horn and dragged them to the edge of the shaft.

He was careful. If there was any

timbering below it would be rotted. The mouth could cave. He lengthened the rope, took the horse around to the far side, pulled the bodies to the edge. The edge held under their weight. He flipped the rope free, found a broken branch, used it as a pry first on the big redhead, then on the smaller man. They disappeared into the hole. From the resonance of the splashes Lassiter judged that the mine was deeply flooded.

12

THIRTY miles out of Nacozari Lassiter quit traveling by daylight. They laid over, deep in a thicket of greasewood, until dark came, moved on through the starlight, and midway through the second night came into the town. A dog barked, another ran snarling at Lassiter's bare heels where he trotted behind the burro. He had come a thousand miles, and if he never walked another step it would be too far.

The night was heavy with cloud. The town showed no light. There was nothing here to tempt a man out of his house after dark. It was safer for the natives to keep behind barred doors, and when the scalp hunters were in from the hills they spent the time behind Streeter's walls with cards and pulque enough to drown them asleep in his patio.

Since the fight at the oasis, Raphael had decided that he owed his life to Lassiter and elected himself his protector. Until then it had not mattered to him what became of the man sent by Huie. He had said.

"I'll take you to my cousin, Juan. He will know where you can find Blood."

"The man I want is named Elkhorn."

"Juan will know about him too. He is Streeter's major-domo."

"Fine. What happend when Streeter hears I'm here?"

Raphael's chuckle was small. "He will not hear it from Juan's household. There's no love between my people and the bounty hunters."

"But he does work for them."

"He has many mouths to feed."

Raphael brought them in by the people's highway, through the back alleys. His knock created some ruckus indoors but not enough to rouse curiosity in the neighbors. Juan took them in through the shed kitchen to the single room that sheltered his fat wife, a clutch of children and two goats. The smell of the goats was lost in the crowd of other odors.

The wife fed them bean and hot peppers while the children watched with huge, sleepy eyes. Lassiter guessed that they would go hungry because he ate. He ate in silence, letting Raphael make the introductions needed to enlist Juan's help. His guide was eloquent. The battle at the oasis became an engagement of magificence. His stamina at crossing the Sierra became a matter for marvel. Juan admitted at last that he was willing to help this one white man. He drove the children and the woman back to bed on the mats around the floor, took his guests to the kitchen for privacy and brought down the gourd of pulque.

They sat crosslegged on the dirt floor. Juan listened to the questions about Streeter, Blood, Elkhorn, then shrugged his contempt. They were all at Streeter's house, he said. All the others were out in the hills looking for Lassiter. The three stayed close, waiting for word that he had been found.

Lassiter said, "Elkhorn is keeping a child down here, a little girl. What do you know about her?"

"The little Loli. The tassel of ripe corn that blows in the wind. The sunlight that dances on the water. Yes, she is in the house, too."

"You make her sound happy. What is she to Elkhorn? How does he treat her?"

"Like any woman. She has a happy heart." Juan's dark face wrinkled with a thought that pleased him. "Her tender fingers have hold of his guts. He is like a Chihuahua puppy when she pulls."

Lassiter drank from his gourd. "Does she come out of the house? If I picked her up would Elkhorn try to get her back?"

"She stays in the house or the patio when he's here. When he goes she stays with the Padre. Streeter leaves

160

the church alone."

"How can I get to her?"

Blankness wiped across Juan's face. "What do you want with her?" The kitchen filled with hostility.

Lassiter said, "Only for a decoy. I want Elkhorn. I won't hurt her."

Juan looked at his cousin. Raphael was nodding reassurance. The man of Nacozari hesitated, had a slow, thoughtful drink from his own gourd, looked at his cousin again to make sure. Then he flung his hands over his shoulders, casting caution away.

"Raphael says tell you. All right. Long back, in the time of the priests, they lived in that house. There was a tunnel under the plaza to take them to the church."

Quiet laughter tightened Lassiter's stomach. It did not show.

"Is it still there or have the earthquakes blocked it?"

"Quien sabe? I know where it starts, where it ends. What is between I don't know. They say the ghosts live there. I have never been in it."

"Anybody you know of been through it?"

Wariness overcame Juan again. Raphael was impatient with his country relative, touched Lassiter's arm confidentially.

"Ten or so years back some people came with a map. They wanted to look in there for treasure they thought the priests hid. They went down, but they didn't come back. The Indos didn't like them digging in sacred ground."

"I won't be doing any digging. Will you show me the church entrance?"

"All right. Si. Raphael says so. We should go now, while the Padre is asleep."

"In a minute." Lassiter stopped him with a hand. He got up, went to the pack that he had dropped beside the door. Over his shoulder he said, "Raphael, I'll bet you can put on a convincing act when you want to, and there's money in it for both of you."

When he turned back to them

162

they were grinning like embarrassed children.

He carried a belt back from the pack, tossed it on the ground between them, watched their eyes widen. It was broad, tooled leather. The belt itself was handsome. The heavy buckle was unique, gold, beaten out by a native smith. The letter L was worked in its center and the letter studded with twenty-four diamonds.

"A lot of people know this belt. They know I'd have to be dead to let go of it. Now . . . " he touched the buckle with his toe, sat down again on his legs, talked out the play for the next day.

★ ★ ★

Before the morning sun got too hot Streeter, with Elkhorn and Blood, had a breakfast in the patio. Streeter baited them, laying bets that Lassiter would get through the scalp hunters watching the trails, amused at Elkhorn's nervousness.

163

Juan brought strong coffee, stood on one foot and then another until Streeter looked to see what was keeping him there. Juan's smile was hesitant.

"Por favor, a word with you, patron?"

Streeter was in a rare good humour. "Shoot. What's your problem?"

"My cousin . . . from Minaca . . . "

"What's he want, a job?"

"No, patron. He has something to sell. Something he found with the American he guided across the mountains."

Blood turned his head, coffee exploding from his mouth. "What American."

Juan spread his hands, looked quickly back to Streeter. "The American had a fight and was killed. He did not need the belt then, so my cousin took it. The buckle is gold, with diamonds. It is worth something, but he does not know where to sell it in Nacozari . . . where they will not cheat him."

Blood's voice struck at him like a gunshot. "Where is he?"

Juan jumped. "Waiting in the kitchen, Senor."

"Get him out here. Now."

Juan went off crabwise, a picture of abject hurry. Streeter looked curious.

"What's the excitement?"

Blood could not sit still. He got up, walked around washing his hands.

"Lassiter had a buckle like that made for him by a goldsmith in Weaverville. It's a big joke up there that the diamonds came from a San Francisco robbery. He did it to mock me."

Elkhorn snorted. "He wasn't wearing anything like that on the Harmony job. I'd have seen it."

Blood threw him a curdling glance. "He's not idiot enough to wear it in a place like Orillo." He tried to cool himself. "Anyway, there are other gold and diamond buckles."

But he still watched the kitchen door. And when Juan led a trembling Raphael into the patio he jumped to meet them.

"Where is it? Where's the belt?"

Raphael looked scared. It wasn't all acting. His eyes ran around over Streeter, Elkhorn, and back to Blood. His hands dropped the conical hat clutched against his stomach, fumbled in the blouse, pulled out the belt. The diamonds shot blue shafts in the sunlight. Blood's breath went in through his teeth noisily. The hand he reached out shook. He took hold of the buckle, felt of its reality.

"It is. This is it. Where the hell did you get this?"

Raphael dropped the end of the belt, swung as if to run. Blood grabbed the back of his shirt, spun him back.

Raphael turned, grovelling. "I didn't kill him Senor. Jesus my witness I didn't kill him."

"Where'd you get it?"

Streeter's laugh came across. "You're scaring the wits out of him. Shut up a minute." He changed to a soft, friendly Spanish. "You aren't going to get hurt. Just say where you got the belt."

Raphael appealed to him. "You will buy it. No?"

"Sure. Be fun to have it. I'll give you a hundred pesos."

Raphael wrenched loose from Blood, dodged by him and kneeled in front of Streeter, caught up his hand and kissed it.

"Gracias. Gracias."

Streeter yanked his hand free, embarrassed. He pulled a leather pouch, spilled out a hundred pesos into Raphael's upturned hand. Raphael scurried toward the kitchen door, close by Blood. Blood caught his arm. Raphael cringed.

Blood's smile was not part of his face. "Boy, I'll give you another hundred if you'll tell me where the body is."

"It was not my fault, Senor."

"Never mind. Never mind. Just, what happened? Where did it happen?"

"At an oasis. El Napal."

Blood called to Streeter over his shoulder. "You know where that is?"

"In a canyon about four days south.

167

Used to be a ranch with a mine."

Blood's fingers were white around the buckle. "Who was the man you were guiding?"

"Quien sabe? He hired me to bring him here."

Blood shook him. "Go on, damn it."

"It is a hard road, Senor."

"So?"

"We turned off to rest at the stream. We shot a deer. We were cooking the liver when the other man came in."

Blood fought for a professional patience, found that it escaped him. "What man was that?"

Ralph slid his eyes toward Streeter. His voice was a bare breath. "I think an Apache hunter."

"One of yours." Blood raised his voice to Streeter, lowered it again for Raphael. "What did he do?"

"Held his rifle on my American. He said the hair was worth five hundred dollars . . . Is the price raised, Senor?"

168

Blood swore at him. "He killed your man then?"

"I didn't see, Senor. I ran behind a rock. I heard two guns. Then nothing. When I looked, carefully, the one is just falling out of his saddle onto my man, who is down. Both of their faces are shot away."

"Killed each other." It was Blood's prayer of thanks. Then training, caution came. "Take me out there. I want to look at him. Maybe you just stole the belt and dreamed up the story."

Raphael moaned and launched into excuses. "It is too late. Senor, I was afraid I would be blamed. I took the horse and dragged the bodies to the old mine and dropped them in the shaft."

"First you took this belt though? Went through their pockets too, I'll bet."

Raphael hung his head. "I had not been paid. I am poor, Senor. I have ten children. All of the truth is this. The belt was not on my American. It was in his pack."

169

Streeter cawed. The shrill sound made Blood's neck hairs raise, but he was not going to be sidetracked. He lowered his face close to Raphael's.

"With that much on your lousy conscience I'll give you a penance to do. You're going to take me out there and fish up those bodies. I'm not taking your word for any of this."

"Yes, Senor." Raphael groaned miserably. "I will do it."

Blood shoved him away. "Let's go."

"We must have mules. We should have a mozo."

"Get them, damn it. Move."

Raphael skittered for the kitchen. He did not let go his giggles until he was back at Juan's with Lassiter. When he was sobered enough he went for animals and a friend of Juan's, a silent man, strong, stupid, without curiosity.

Blood drove the party. It took them less than three days to find the fertile canyon. To Blood the fishing with grappling hooks seemed to take longer. They brought up the smaller man first.

The body was not easily identifiable even if it had had a face.

Blood walked around it, studying. The size should have been about right, judging by the clothes. The hair on the backs of the hands was within Lassiter's color range.

"You're sure this is the man you brought over the mountains?"

Raphael was sure.

"Let's get the other one up."

"It is nearly dark, Senor."

"So build a fire."

They built a fire beside the shaft, and fished. Both of the Indos showed growing nervousness. The mozo was whining.

"A bad place. A bad place."

Raphael finally threw down the rope. "We cannot find him. Senor, let's put this one back in the water. If he is not burned he will walk at night."

Blood cursed all superstition, but even under the threat of his gun the mozo stood like a bull, shaking his head. He would do nothing more until

171

morning. Blood gave up and turned in for the night.

The whistling of quail waked him. He rolled out of his blanket and shouted at the Indos. It frightened the quail but nothing else. Both men were gone. So were the mules.

13

STREETER sat on in the patio after Blood had gone rushing off like a baying hound on the trail. Elkhorn amused him. He was torn two ways. He wanted to go with Blood, be sure the man he had set up was dead, and he was sweating to get Miguel's pack train headed for Tombstone. Streeter taunted him.

"The fat man sold you out. You still going to run his errands?"

Elkhorn was bellicose. "I don't believe he did. Blood says so, but I don't trust Blood. I think he was just conning us into nailing Lassiter for him . . . what do you think . . . is Lassiter really dead?"

Streeter stood up with the jeweled belt. "I'd guess so." He fitted the leather around his waist, admiring it. "This thing ought to cost a couple of thousand American, huh? Yeah, I'd say he was dead."

"Then I'm cutting out. I've lost plenty, playing poker down here. I need the money coming to me for that train."

Streeter shrugged. He guessed the Don would get plenty for what was in that train, but it was nothing to him. He didn't intend to hit it and bring down a hornet's nest on Nacozari. So long as Apaches hung around the hills he and his men made enough off the Mexican authorities.

Elkhorn was saying, "I'm going to go tell Jake to have things ready to move out at sunset."

Before he left the patio he ran up the outside stairs to the balcony, along it to the room where the kid was. He came back, disgruntled, said, "Out like a lamp. Damn her," hesitated, then went through the gate, pushed by the urgency to be leaving here.

He had never left the girl in the house alone before.

Streeter smoked a cigarette, looking up at the balcony. Then he tossed it away, went up the stairs. The balcony ran around all four sides of the patio. The bedrooms, long, narrow cells, opened on it in the Spanish style. The priests had liked their privacy. Streeter went straight to the girl's room. His boot heels clacked on the tile floor. He opened the door.

The odor of peyote came at him. The kid had been chewing mescal buttons. He went in and closed the door. The cool light from the high window fell across her, on the bed. Like Elkhorn had said, she was out cold. Her face was pale against the bright red blanket under her. Her young lips smiled with whatever her dream was. Long, pale hair covered part of her face and blouse. The full Indian skirt covered her legs to her ankles.

Streeter's loins burned. He went to the bed, put a hand under her, pulled the blouse over her head, pulled off the skirt. He had never seen her without

175

clothes before He looked at her closely. She really was a kid. Just beginning to develop. She was good to look at, but now she was like a strip of limp bacon. She was no good to him that way. He wanted some life, some fire, a fight. He went out and spent the day waiting.

Elkhorn came back. They played poker, head and head because nobody else was there to make a game. The sun went down. Shadows filled the patio. An Indian woman brought candles, then food. They ate, then Elkhorn got up.

"The pack train's ready. I'll see you next trip." He started for the stairs.

Streeter said, "Where you going?"

"For Loli."

"Not this time."

Elkhorn's mouth dropped. "What do you mean?"

"This time she stays here."

"The hell. She's mine."

Streeter eased his gun out of the holster, laid it on the table, kept his hand on it. His eyes caught the red glint of the candles.

"You good enough to take her?"

A scream came up through Elkhorn. He wanted to yell, to curse. He wanted to draw, kill Streeter. He didn't have the nerve. He knew it. He stood, feeling his legs drain. Then all the frustration that had ridden his life, the fear, the hatred of those who could do what he could not, whipped around him like a cat-o'-nine-tails. He fled through the gate.

Streeter sat, drinking sparingly, listening until the servants were gone. He would not have them in the house at night. He heard the rear gate close. Then he climbed the stairs.

* * *

The day dragged for Lassiter. He could not leave the one room of Juan's mud house, could not escape the flock of children that raced in and out, their screeching bickering games. The smaller ones ran naked, wiry little brown bodies with a built-in resistance to the sun to make a white man jealous. It was like being in a nest of baby spiders. Juan's wife was a placid blob, paying no attention to the turmoil around her. She set the pot of beans beside the fire where it would keep warm, and through the hours there was always one or another thin brown arm dipping into it. Beyond that she gave no time to maternal chores. She was busy, combing out *pita* fibres.

Lassiter watched her, thinking about the largesse of the plant from which they came. Corn, beans, mouth blistering chilis, they were the staples of the country. But the maguey, the maguey was life. It gave with an open hand. The broad, thick sword leaves bordered with stabbing spines: the thick, tough stalk thrusting out of the middle toward the sky: the delicate white bell flowers at the top, and then the hard shelled pod of seeds. Everything had its use. The fibres, twisted into strands, woven, made snares for the trapping of birds, seines with which to fish the river, ropes for a thousand purposes. The sap, collected when the young flower stalk shot up, fermented into mescal, pulque. You could get drunk enough on pulque to forget the raw realities. And when the pulque was not enough there were the peyote, the ripe seed buttons to chew. There was escape in the buttons. Chewing them made you ten feet tall. They brought dreams. Colors you have never seen before. Marvels you had never known. You could fly above the earth like a bird. Live under the water with the fish. With the buttons came wisdom. Peace. Beauty. Kinship with the gods. The maguey kept the people going.

Juan came in before sundown. Elkhorn had been out somewhere, but he was back in the house, playing cards with Streeter. The girl was alone in the room, Juan told Lassiter how to reach it.

After midnight, when the town was asleep, the Padre asleep, Juan led

Lassiter along the dark street, entered the church by a small side door, moved down the nave and came before the altar.

The altar was built of massive stones cut and fitted without mortar. At the back was one stone that looked like all the others. It wasn't. Juan stood back, not wanting to touch it himself, directing Lassiter to push on it in specific places. When he pushed the last place the stone moved, slid inward, pivoted. The old priests had brought the craft from a country long practiced in stone work, had taught their slave masons well. Juan held a candle, lit a second one from it, handed it to Lassiter.

The wavering flame threw light on a flight of worn stone steps going down into the ground below the church. Air oozed up, dusty, hot, dead. Lassiter wondered whether enough fresh air would replace it to let him breathe. He waited, allowing some time for it to penetrate.

Juan pointed out a lever inside that controlled the pivot stone. Lassiter stepped through, went down the steps. The passage was narrow, only five feet high. He walked bent over, ducking the roof. Underfoot dust made a thick carpet. There were no footprints. No one had been here for many years.

Wherever there was a church in this country there were rumours of such tunnels. Old stories insisted that at the time of the Indian uprising the priests had hidden the gold chalices, the silver vessels, all that the white men considered valuable, in these tunnels. Many of them had been discovered, but if anything had been found it was shrouded in secrecy. Perhaps there was a treasure here, perhaps someone unknown had found the way in and succeeded in robbing the place. Perhaps he would come across their bones, or the dust of them.

The candle flame waved as new air went past it. The shadows mocked that anything was alive here. At intervals a cut stone had fallen from the roof. Dried tree roots groped out of the holes, withered at not finding water.

The passage curved, and beyond he came up against a shoulder of rubble that almost filled the tunnel. It had caved here a long time ago. At the top was a space, but not deep enough to wriggle through. He studied the hanging roof, then set the candle against the wall and pulled rocks down from the pile. He put them aside carefully, not to jar the floor, not to shake anything more down from the top.

With an hour he had a crevice big enough to force his shoulders through. He went into it. If the roof fell now he would be wedged under it. He would smother there or be slowly crushed. His shirt was sweat through. Dirt clung to it, moved with him. There was sudden pressure as his shoulder brushed the roof, a rock came down between his shoulders. He lurched ahead. More weight fell on his ankles, pinned them.

Panic reached for him. He put all of his strength into the leverage of his arms and pulled forward. Gradually, gradually he dragged free. He slithered down the far side of the pile.

The hole filled behind him with a thundering fall of earth. Whatever was ahead, he could not come back this way.

He ran. Blackness constricted around him like a boa. He stumbled, went to his knees. His knees struck the edge of a step, sent pain through him. He felt ahead. There were stairs going up. He crawled until his head hit stone. In the dark it took him another ten minutes' search with his fingers to locate the wooden bar that would release the slab above him.

When it gave he was dripping wet. The warm night air struck cold against him. He pushed upward on the stone, looked up at stars that rushed away from him.

They threw silver light into the patio. He stood orienting himself. Juan had said there would be nobody in the house except Streeter, Elkhorn and the girl, Debbie's daughter. Elkhorn and the girl would be in the one room, Streeter at the other side of the house. He did not want to wake Streeter. He wanted to take Elkhorn out, get the truth of the Harmony story from him. What he did then would depend on the answers Elkhorn gave him.

Earlier he had planned to use the girl. Now he didn't need her. Now she was in the way. He couldn't take the chance that she would make noise.

He brushed dirt from his trousers, polished his hands dry on them, worked the grit from between his fingers, tested his grip for comfort. He drew his knife in his right hand; a knife was quiet. He took his gun in his left, for insurance, and went cat footed up the stairs.

He stopped at the door, his mouth set. There was sound inside. Music. A soft guitar. Light seeped under the door. There was no other entrance to the room. He knew how Spanish rooms were built, one door, one window at the second story level. He opened the door quickly.

A glance told him that only the two people were there. On the bed. He turned the gun that way.

The girl sat Indian fashion on the foot of the bed, her naked back to him, bent over the guitar. She picked the strings. The music was wispy, wandering, a forlorn sound, forlorn as the long pale hair that hung down around her.

The naked man lay propped against pillows, his head back, his eyes closed, facing Lassiter. Lassiter had backed against the door, closing it, before the man sat up. He sat up fast, throwing one bare leg toward the floor. He was on the way to launching himself in a flying, furious dive. Then he saw the gun. He stopped.

It was not Elkhorn. It was someone Lassiter had not seen before. It could only be Streeter.

Lassiter raised his voice above the

185

whine of the strings. "Where's Elkhorn?"

Streeter looked at him, wholly still. He was a scrawny body, matted with hair, the flesh where it showed, spare, cross-hatched with white scars from old knife cuts. The eyes were sharp, steady, the predatory eyes of an eagle.

The guitar kept on in its floundering rhythm.

After a time Streeter said, "You must be Lassiter."

"Where's Elkhorn?"

"Not here."

Lassiter took one step forward. "Where?"

The outer corners of the eagle eyes wrinkled. Streeter's tension appeared to ease. He was not relaxing. He was adjusting his balance, loosening his shoulders.

"Gone north." Streeter made a sudden grab for the girl.

She was like lightning. She rolled, spinning off the far edge of the bed. His fingers caught at her flying hair, could not hold it. The strands slid through, raised up, waving. She pirouetted away, stripping her nails across the guitar in a loud, sharp discord, fell into a weaving backward dance following a quick ripple of notes, a childhood skipping step. Lassiter's eyes flickered after her.

In the instant they were off him, Streeter moved. He left the bed in a leap. It took him to the chair where his gun belt hung. Lassiter fired. He missed. Streeter fired twice. Lassiter had never met a man this fast. The first shot clubbed his gun out of his hand, paralyzed it. The second bored a groove along the side of his skull above his ear. The force knocked him down. Somewhere in the room the guitar was playing.

He lay doggo. Streeter's bare footsteps padded toward him, stopped above him. The man's laugh was confident. He thought Lassiter was dead. Lassiter lay on his side. He felt Streeter's hand on his fingers, taking the knife. He let it go, snapped his hand around, caught the wrist and yanked. Streeter toppled over him, caught by surprise. Lassiter jackknifed, spinning on his knees, threw himself at the arm with which Streeter was bringing up his gun. He fell on it, twisting it, got one knee on the elbow, broke the arm backward.

Streeter shouted, raised his legs and wrapped them around Lassiter. He had the wiry strength to throw him sidewise, to claw with his good hand at Lassiter's face, reaching for the eyes.

Lassiter's head was ringing, his reactions slowed by the blow of the bullet. He turned in time to take Streeter's rigid two fingers on his cheeks instead of in the eye sockets. He dug his hands into the mat of hair on the bare chest, hauled it up, slammed it against the floor. Streeter's head hit hard. Before he moved again Lassiter found the butt of the gun Streeter had dropped. He brought the barrel down on Streeter's head as he was raising it. He heard the skull break. Streeter dropped back and lay still, going slack. There was no emphasis, no punctuation in the melody of the guitar, only the plaintive, wistful, clear, individual notes.

Lassiter stayed astraddle of Streeter, fighting down grogginess. He touched the side of his head. It was wet with blood. Blood made a sponge of his hair. He wiped his hand across his shirt, joggled Streeter's gun into a more solid grip, sank back on his haunches, looked around the room.

The girl sat cross legged on the blue tiles, not in the middle of the room but well out from the walls. Her head was bent over the guitar in her lap, tilted, as if she listened to sounds only she could hear, listened to the music as it was transmuted into the golden sounds of her peyote dream.

Lassiter got up. His first steps were unsteady. He caught at the corner of the bed, called up steadiness, felt it seep through him. Then he went to the girl.

"Loli."

She lifted her face slowly. Her fingers picked on at the strings. Her eyes followed up his legs, over his body, settled on his mouth. She did not speak.

"Loli. Can you hear me?"

A slow nod.

"Do you know where Elkhorn went?"

Another nod.

"Where?"

Very slowly her eyes searched all the corners of the room. They touched on Streeter briefly, passed on, to the door. Some words came in a light, bodiless voice. The only one he could make out was *north*.

He put a finger under her chin, lifted it. The vague eyes seemed to try to focus.

"Through Nogales?"

The head moved to one side.

"Agua Prieta?"

The head moved back.

"Camino Real?"

The head moved to both sides.

190

"Then how?"

The lips moved but the sound didn't mean anything.

"Do you know how he went?"

She tried again to speak, could not. She nodded. Then she giggled. Her eyes went up to his. And crossed. And closed. Loli went to sleep.

14

LASSITER found his belt, that he had not expected to see again. He found the girl's blouse, the skirt, in the tangle of the bed. He worked them onto the limp little figure, left the girl on the floor, went to look down into the patio. There was no movement. Apparently Juan was right that there was no one else in the house. The shots had not caused any attention. He went inside, collected his gun and knife, hung the girl over his shoulder, on impulse picked up the guitar, and left the house.

Juan answered his knock on the rear door, saw the bloody head, the girl's rump, and said nothing. He made a signal not to wake the children, the wife sleeping in the front room, backed to let Lassiter enter. Lassiter kept his voice a whisper.

"Did you get the horses?"

"Si. Elkhorn?"

"He got away. I don't know when he left, but Streeter was with the girl. I killed him. I think she knows where Elkhorn went but she'll have to sleep off the peyote before she can tell me."

Juan brought a blanket to the kitchen. Lassiter laid the girl on it and sat down, let Juan work on the gash in his head, plaster it with a grease that he insisted would keep poison out.

Lassiter sat until an hour before daylight, smoking, not sleeping. He watched the girl and let his mind wonder about her. She was not like the Indian or Mexican girls, who were woman at thirteen. She still had the figure and face of childhood. But she was a child of the border. He did not know how long she had been with Elkhorn, how he had used her. But his first look at her, naked on the bed, Streeter beside her looking as if he had eaten a canary, told him enough. She had reason to chew peyote. Childhood had been short for her. The corner of his lip tucked in. He heard Debbie, in Orillo, talking about Blood's promise to get the two of them to San Francisco. Even if he kept that promise it was too late for Debbie. And it was too late for Loli. And Blood knew it.

He let her sleep until the little hands began to clench, jerk as the drug wore off, as reality crept into her unconsciousness. Then he waked her. She waked immediately, with that holdover from childhood, instant orientation. She looked him over openly, curiously, then settled her shoulders back on the blanket. She startled him by smiling.

Lassiter backed off.

"You said you knew which way Elkhorn went. Is that true?"

She was as startled as he. She shrugged and sat up, nodding.

"Tell me."

"I don't know how to tell it." The voice was still light, without body.

"What do you mean?"

"I've gone that way with him when he took the train, but I don't know the names of the turns."

"Could you show me?"

The eyes brightened. "A trip? Sure."

He roused Juan to saddle the horses, load the packs. He paid the Indo twice what he'd expected. That was an old habit. It left along his trail pools of friendship that he might call on again. Part of his pattern of the unexpected.

The hills were still dark but the sky grayed as they rode north. The trail was narrow but used. He guessed that it was a smugglers' trail, and that took his mind to Elkhorn's train. He rode abreast of the girl and asked if she knew what the man was carrying.

"The usual goods. Gold, opium, Chinese girls for the houses there."

"Where's there?"

"Tombstone first. Then he goes down to Orillo with money for Don Miguel." She looked at him and with

195

a new curiosity. "Why do you want him?"

"He tried to get me hung. I want to know why."

"And then I guess you'll kill him?"

He looked at her, not answering.

She rode a little while, silent. Then, "After you find him you won't need me any more. What are you going to do with me?"

He began an answer, stopped. "What do you want me to do?"

She surveyed him as if she were buying him. "Keep me with you." She saw his eyes, hurried on. "I know more than the Chinese girls. More than anybody. Don Miguel taught me everything. Keep me. Just for yourself."

That he could not do. His time for keeping a woman with him was far past. A wife or any woman associated with him would make him that much more vulnerable. He could never stay in one place, put down roots. He could not give Blood or the others on his back trail any purchase, any handhold by which to pull him down.

He shook his head, impatient. She did not wheedle at least. She dug her heels into the horse and rode ahead, turned in at a branch track up through the rising hills.

He did not know how much headstart Elkhorn had. At least the night if he had ridden through it. But the two horses could make better time than a string of burros, especially with them carrying human freight. If he had camped they would overhaul him quicker.

His head hurt. His hat pressed against the raw wound, made it throb. His skull felt like it was swelling. As the sun went up the sky its heat nauseated him. Then chills shook him. Dizziness started in his stomach, raged up, spun through his brain. Sometime near noon he raised his eyes to look at the barrier of mountains they were climbing toward. The crest wheeled, slow at first, then faster. The horizon turned black, leaving an after-vision of silhouette against the white sky. He floated in the spinning silence. After a long while brilliant colored lights exploded.

Consciousness came back furtively. He grew aware of feeling. Sharp hardness under him. He was on the ground. He was warm, warm against his stomach. The inside of his head was swimming in a tilting circle. He opened his eyes on blackness. He moved his head and stars reeled around him. He closed his eyes against the dizziness. His arm rested on a warm body. He moved it, drew it in, found that the girl had curled herself close against him. A blanket lay over them both. He tried to move but the dizziness swept through him. He blanked out again.

When he woke again it was mid-morning and the sun burned his eyes. He was thirsty, his mouth dry, his lips swollen. The girl was not beside him. He tried to sit up, instead rolled onto his stomach, caught himself on his elbows. Squinting, he looked at what was around him. He saw the horses up the slope, tied to the thick center mast of a maguey plant. The mast was dead, broken half way up, the top hanging from the break, the stiff flower branches caught in a bush ten feet away. Downgrade there was a rockburst, the flame of a fire at its base. The girl was there. Hot as the day was she fed the blaze. A can hung above it was steaming. The steam rolled slowly, in time with the low voice of the guitar.

He made a sound. She looked up. He touched his mouth, wanting water. Instead of the canteen she brought a cup poured from the can. When she kneeled with it he batted it away. Her chin set and she brought another cup of the hot liquid. He could smell it. He knew what it was. She had made a tea of the maguey buttons. Peyote. He was too weak, needed water too much to refuse it this time. She held it against his lips and he drank it. He tried to fight to his feet and could not make it.

199

She looked scared but determined. He heard the light voice. "Go to sleep. Go to sleep. Go to sleep."

The dreams began. For him they were not pretty, peaceful dreams. They did not make him smile. When he waked again it was another night. He was exhausted. He welcomed the warmth of the small body wedged against him. She was not asleep. He felt her tension, her trembling at the sound of prowling animals. He tightened his arm around her, then released her.

"Go build up the fire. They won't come around a fire."

She left him and he slept again. In the morning his head was clear but he was too weak to ride. He crawled back against the branches and watched the girl.

She had her fire going, a can of beans hanging over it. She brought him coffee, weak but hot, left the pot beside him, went back to the pack and dug out a sack of ground corn. She mixed it into a dough, rolled a wad of it into a ball, tucked a corner of her skirt into her waist, beat the dough ball out to a pancake shape against her bare hip. She used a stick to clear the fire and ash off the top of a flat rock, dropped the tortilla on it and shaped another. When she had a stack of them cooked she dished out two plates of beans, gathered the tortillas in her skirt, hooked it into a sack using the hem to pick up the plates, and climbed to him. She sat beside him, gave him one plate, spread her legs to make a serving cloth and scooped beans into her mouth. She chewed earnestly, casting a slanting look at him.

"I guess I don't cook very good."

Lassiter agreed. But it was food, and he needed strength. He ate the whole serving and when she quit eating he finished the tortillas.

She cleaned up the vessels in the manner of a child, a sketchy gesture, wiping them out with sand, dropping them beside the fire for further use. She turned away from chores, went for her guitar and lost herself in it.

Lassiter walked away, out of reach of the sound. He spent the day trying to strengthen his legs, alternately moving and resting. By night, he thought, he would be able to travel.

By night Loli was deep in peyote dreams. He tried but could not rouse her. He stripped off her blouse and skirt, heard the hard buttons tucked into her waistband rattle on the sand, dressed her again and moved her out of reach of the seed pods. Without her to guide him he had no choice but to spend another night here. And where was Elkhorn?

He slept and roused before daylight, and shook the girl awake. As she opened her eyes he shook her harder.

"You put one more of those things in your mouth while you're with me and I'll take the hide off of you. I know you can find them all along the trail. Just don't pick them up."

She acted as if he had already whipped her. He got her into the saddle, pulled his horse in behind her and shoved up the trail. It was mid-day before his anger left him, before he admitted that the drug was the only thing the doleful figure ahead of him had to support her. But he could not afford to have her steeped in its hallucinations now.

"I'll give you a bushel of them later," he told her. From the way she brightened he might have promised her the moon.

★ ★ ★

They pushed through the mountains, up through the old Perez Grant, crossed the border east of Agua Prieta. Once there had been a presidio manned by Spanish soldiers for control of Indian marauders. They passed the ruins of the buildings, the crumbling walls of the 'dobe church. Farther north they crossed a series of deep ruts left by the wagons of the gold trains headed for California, trying a southern route. He thought she was aiming for Guadalupe Canyon, which would take them eastward into New Mexico. Instead she turned west, keeping to the most empty land.

They saw Tombstone many miles before they came to it. A lion's paw of light stretched across the high mesa, reaching down from the silver lode in the hills. He had not been in the area for five years. The town had not existed then. Now it was a metropolis. Fifteen thousand people. A queen city sprouted in the middle of a brutal wilderness. He knew its reputation. The saloons along Allen and Tough Nut Street never closed. A river of silver changed hands across the gambling tables. The bars served murderers, holdup men, rustlers, mine owners, Senators alike.

The roaring noise of the streets made everything he had heard believable. He had glimpses of the crowds, of the lights that drove back the desert night, but the girl bypassed the center of the town. She circled behind the Bird

Cage theater, winding through the back alleys of the red light district past the crib rows, into the Chinese section that huddled around the josh houses. There were no lights here. The darkness made it a place to expect attack. A drunk wandering back here would be robbed, beaten, murdered in the space of a minute. It was a stinking sink, the closest thing like it the Barbary Coast of San Francisco.

Lassiter rode with his gun in his hand. Three times black shapes ran at them out of the shadows. He clubbed them down. He did not want to fire, to bring the gibbering Chinese tumbling out of the ratholes around him. He wanted no chance of losing his guide this near the end of his search.

She rode close against him, hunched down, trying to make herself invisible. They reached a corner where some glow from the bright street seeped in. She stopped at a building different from the others, with a two story hexagonal tower lifting out of the squalid street.

The walls had no windows, only a single heavy door with a dragon etched in gold across its top. The light did not reach in here. There was movement. Darker shadows slipped forward without sound. Lassiter sat still. The horses were surrounded by figures that he could not see, a circle of solid, black shapes.

The girl had whispered a name as they turned in at the yard. Lassiter used Cantonese to ask for him.

"Is the honorable Chang How at home?"

A shape taller than the others materialized at his bridle. "I don't know your voice. Who are you?"

"From Weaverville. From Ho Ling."

The tall shape melted into the others. There was a time of waiting, of silence, then the figure was at the bridle again. Lassiter had neither seen nor heard a door open or close.

"Chang How bids you welcome to his humble abode. Step down, both of you. I will take you to him."

The other shadows parted to let them pass. It was hard to know that they were really there. Lassiter took the girl's arm, followed the tall shape to a corner of the yard. At the base of the wall the black figure reached for Lassiter's hand, tugged it lightly, led them down steps that went into the earth. At the bottom he left them, climbed again and quietly lowered a trap door over their heads. Only then did he light a torch. In its yellow glow Lassiter saw the long blade of a knife in the guide's free hand. The face was long for an Oriental, the black eyes opaque.

The passage was close, heavy with incense blended with other odors. It ran for sixty feet. Lassiter paced it, unconsciously measuring. At the end a flight of skeleton stairs took them up, into a narrow hall. Up there the smell of opium cooking in the tiny bowls of long pipes was strong, sickening. The hall led to a plank door. The guide opened it, stood aside, ushered them into another world.

The room was low ceilinged, the walls hidden behind heavy silk hangings bright with a multitude of woven figures. On a black lacquer dais a porcelain Buddha smiled enigmatically over the pudgy hands clasped against the fat white belly. Their feet were sunk deep in the thick pile of a blue Chinese rug. The guide closed the door, left them alone in the room.

Loli stared, wide-eyed, frightened by the opulence. She whispered.

"I've never been in here before. It looks so rich for a heathen place."

"Rich indeed, in this beggarly land."

They had not heard him come in. He was small, very old, but the yellow face was smooth, like a weathered hazel nut. His queue was wrapped in a knot on top of his head, covered by a black cap topped with the red button of a Mandarin first class. Lassiter doubted that the Chinese had the right to wear even the worked silver button of the ninth grade kwan. He wore a robe embroidered with the figure of the Mandarin crane. Certainly he considered himself a being of importance. He bowed formally to Lassiter.

"Laie tells me you have come from Ho Ling?"

Lassiter unfastened the handsome belt, turned the diamond studded buckle over, extended it, exhibited the engraving on the back.

"He made this for me. You know his mark?"

The small Chinese sucked air through his teeth. His hands were folded into the hanging sleeves of his robe. He drew one out, reached a finger to touch the buckle. The fingernails were inches long, guarded by steel claws fitted onto the fingertips.

"Yes. That is Ho Ling. Why does he send you?"

"I'm looking for a smuggler who brought goods to you a few days ago. Elkhorn."

The black, watchful eyes did not change. The face was bland, without expression. "Does Ho Ling want him?"

Lassiter tipped his head toward Loli. "This is his girl."

"I know her."

"I'm bringing her back to him."

The small head bowed. "Leave her. She will be taken to him."

"Your pardon, kwan. It's my responsibility."

The Chinese looked up. There was something in his eyes now, a crafty humour.

"You are not Casimero Streeter, who had this belt last week. You are, I think, Lassiter. Elkhorn believes you are dead."

Lassiter's smile was thin. The little Oriental matched it.

"You are not Elkhorn's good friend."

"No."

"Why do you think I would help you find him?"

"He isn't your good friend either, and you don't want trouble. You can't afford it."

"Honorable sir, I have no trouble."

"You can have. Ho Ling has more weight than you. He'll back me."

The Chinese took time to consider. Lassiter followed the running thoughts. How much did Lassiter know? How strong were the man's connection with the tongs of Weaverville? Did he dare kill him and drop him into the lime pit under the building?

Lassiter had heard of the lime pit, among other whispers about Chang How. He played a poker game now with high stakes, his ace his own reputation and the Oriental's vulnerability. He watched Chang How's uncertainty grow, the need to look at the ace.

"If I don't give him to you . . . what?"

Lassiter's smile was a threat, cold, intended. "Your race runs a network of businesses all through the West. Some are within the laws, some aren't. You, Chang How, deal in opium, gambling, girls. I've let your people alone because Ho Ling helped me out once. He and I have an understanding. His men don't interfere with me and I don't touch his places. So far. You could make yourself unpopular. And you have a lot to lose."

The black eyes changed slightly. Lassiter knew that the game was won, but the Chinese are consummate gamblers. Chang How must play the last card out.

"Who knows you are here? You could disappear."

Lassiter did not lift the gun, but let his hand rest of the curved stock plates.

"Not before I can kill you."

"You wouldn't leave here alive."

"That wouldn't help you. Is Elkhorn worth it to you?"

The Chinese bowed.

Elkhorn was sold. Not, as to Don Miguel, for money, but to protect the security with which Chang How's varied treasures moved across the West.

The little man moved with a mincing step, his slippered feet making no sound in the deep rug, crossed to the far wall, pulled on a tasseled cord. The silk drape whispered back. There was a door behind it that swung inward at Chang How's touch. They went into a bare hall, made meaner by the luxury they left behind. Loli hung back, nervous. Lassiter took her arm and guided her ahead of him to the circular stairway, followed the Chinese down. The odor of opium increased. It was overwhelming when the door at the bottom was opened.

The room beyond was lighted by an oil lamp, the air almost opaque with smoke. Through it Lassiter had a dim view of tiers of curtained bunks against the walls. Chang How pulled back the lowest curtain of the near tier. Elkhorn lay there, trail soiled, unshaved, unconscious, a cold pipe in a dish on a small shelf above his shoulder.

Elkhorn. Elkhorn.

But in no condition to answer questions.

Chang How stood back, looking

down on the sunken, sagging face in distaste.

Lassiter said, "Get somebody to carry him out of here."

The Chinese brought a silver bell from his sleeve, shook it lightly. Two men came in at once by a second door, their knives held ready. Lassiter put his fingers on his gun, watched Chang How's eyes, watched for a sign that the man would try an attack. He did not. He was elaborately careful, using English to order Elkhorn taken up the stairs, to the yard.

Lassiter kept hold of the girl, kept close to the kwan. He wanted it understood that in the outer darkness he could still strike down the master of the house before he could be stopped. But this time there was light, a torch that showed the men in black pants and shirts.

Elkhorn's horse was brought, saddled, the limp figure draped on it, tied there. The girl was helped onto her horse. Lassiter took out his gun.

"Get on my horse, Chang How. Tell your crew I'll drop you off when we're clear of town. Tell them not to follow."

There was a tightening among the men. Chang How debated. The muzzle of the gun was steady on his middle. He beckoned for help, had trouble with his robe, his fingernails, was hoisted clumsily onto the horse. Lassiter handed Elkhorn's rein to the girl, stepped up behind Chang How, put the gun against the robe.

"All right, Loli. At a walk."

They went out into the dark alley. Lassiter did not expect a bullet in the back. Not with the kwan sitting in his lap.

A chattering of high Oriental voices swelled behind them. Black shadows ran past them, set up a cry that brought a general yelling. Doors opened and closed quickly. The brief bursts of light showed a scuttling of the baggy figures, emptying the alleys. Lassiter smiled. It was a bonus of security.

The tong making certain that in the blackness the kwan was not attacked by mistake.

They rode without hurry. The last shacks fell behind. The alley disintegrated to a foot trail, swerved and came into the main trail, climbed into the brush cover of the hills. The noise, the brilliance of Tombstone faded, was cut off behind a turn. Lassiter called to the girl, pulled up and dropped to the ground, lifted down the Chinese. The man flinched from the touch of the Occidental hands. Lassiter dug his fingers into the plump shoulder, used pain for emphasis.

"About putting your hatchetmen on my trail, don't do it."

It was a risk he couldn't avoid, leaving the kwan here. His train was too big already. He did not want to haul the Chinese along too. He had made an enemy of the tong, he knew, but he had to chance that Chang How would not want trouble stirred up in his compound. A white man and woman attacked by the yellow people, already held in fear and suspicion, could bring bloody reprisal from the major community.

An hour later he knew that Chang How had taken that chance. He pushed up beside the girl, kept his voice low.

"We're being followed. Take Elkhorn and keep going. I'll catch up."

She didn't want to go on through the night alone. He used his hat to slap her horse, to send it running down the trail. Behind him the whisper of other running horses grew. Six or more. In the open the number wasn't important. He had fought Apaches through these hills. Against them the hatchetmen were clumsy.

He lifted the rifle from under his knee, took a side draw to the crest of a knoll, got down, went in a crouch to where he saw a sweep of the trail below him. They came in a cluster, without care, depending on speed and their knowledge that his horses were tired.

He had learned patience from the

Indians. He held his fire as they came toward him, waited until they were close below him. Then he shot into the group. A yell came back, a horse went down. Two Chinese in an argument sound hysterical; in numbers they sounded like panic. The group broke up, spread, raced for cover in the brush, headed back toward town. He knocked a second man out of his saddle. They were out of sight then, but he knew the doggedness of these people. They would be back, by more devious routes.

He shifted position to watch the hills, saw movement and shot toward it. He drew return fire, bullets that whipped through the rocks around him. He changed his place, listening. He could not see them but he heard them. Now they were trying to get behind him. They weren't hurrying. There would be daylight in awhile. Then he could expect a rush. He eased down the knoll, taking his time, making no sound. The rush would find him gone, watching from another place for them to show themselves.

Shots exploded from the east. He had a sharp picture. Somebody had circled wide to cut his retreat, had run into the girl and Elkhorn. She had probably stopped to wait for him. He cursed, dived for the rock burst where he had left his horse, flung up and broke for the trail.

The horse stumbled, caught itself, made the jump down the last sharp bank. He kicked it, headed east. A batlike shape rose at the trail side, a gun blasted, close. The bullet cut between him and the horse's neck. Then he was abreast, leaning wide, beating his rifle barrel down on the bare head. The head cracked.

He was past. Shots followed him. He swept over a rim, dropped into deeper shadow in a bowl, saw the bulk of a horse down in the trail, a quiet patch of white cloth beside it. That would be the girl.

A diving black streak caught his eye

too late. His leg was grabbed, pulled, he was dragged out of the saddle. There were two of them. A knife blade caught what little light there was, winked, flashed past him as he rolled. The blade snapped against rock. He came up, was jumped on by the second man, threw him over his head into a tangle with his fellow. It was noisy. They scrambled apart. Lassiter swung a boot toe against one head, reached for his gun. He realized that he could see them clearly. Light was coming. They crouched, ready to charge him. He shot them. He watched until they fell and were still. Then he turned to the girl, She sprawled, arms and legs flung out. He would not have time to bury her.

He lifted her, reacted with a start that she was breathing. She weighed hardly enough to put tension on his arms. He found no sign that she had been shot. She must had been knocked out when her horse fell. He stepped into the saddle with her, held her against him in the crook of his arm, saw the tracks of Elkhorn's horse running east along the trail and spurred after them.

He stopped often, watching for pursuit, but the Chinese did not appear again. The girl waked and clung against him. Tears fell on his hand.

The sun was up when they found Elkhorn's horse grazing, skittish as they came up, nervous at the burden wriggling on its back. Elkhorn was conscious, the aftermath of the opium making him retch. His red eyes found Lassiter but he was too sick to be afraid.

15

FEAR came later, after Lassiter had taken them five miles off the trail, sweeping their tracks out until he felt that the hatchetmen could not find where he had left the road.

He found a low ridge of volcanic rock lying like the spine of a prehistoric dragon, a district pitted with shallow caves, many of them stained with the smoke of Indian fires. It was a headquarters area for Indians still living in the hills, but at this season they were higher, up in the timber, collecting berries from the summer crop. Lassiter made a wide sweep, reading signs, making sure. Then he chose a cave that looked down the slope of tumbled rock to the open swale at its base.

Elkhorn was too sick to sit a horse. Lassiter had left him tied across it, taking no notice of the strangling sounds, the weak pleading. Outside the cave he handed the girl down, swung off and carried Elkhorn inside, propped him against the rock wall, built a small fire in the mouth of the hollow.

"Make us some coffee, Loli. Strong."

Elkhorn's head came up. He had not been aware that she was there. He looked from her to Lassiter and the fear came. His mind was too fuddled to make the connection between them, but animal instinct warned him that it had meaning. He made sounds, but his mouth was too dry to form words. Lassiter sat down across the cave, rolled a cigarette and watched Elkhorn. His eyes did not shift from the man's face.

The water boiled. The girl dropped coffee into it, set the pot aside. Lassiter did not move. He waited while the coffee steeped, while its smell filled the cave. Then he settled it with cold water, poured a cup full, put it in

Elkhorn's shaking hands, cut the rope around his wrists. Elkhorn was past trying to use the freedom, past thinking of fight or escape. He held the cup, looking up with little comprehension, the pupils of his eyes contracted to pinpoints. Lassiter said.

"Drink it."

Elkhorn raised the cup, swallowed, retched, spewing the liquid across his feet.

"Again."

The pot was empty before Elkhorn could keep enough down to prime his circulation. The girl made another pot. As Elkhorn's vision cleared his eyes followed her. She would not look his way.

Lassiter let the time run on. Elkhorn would have to dredge up mind enough to know what he was saying before anything could be got out of him. They were a long time coming. They were hoarse, whispered through a graveled throat.

"Loli. How'd she get here?"

Lassiter flipped a cigarette at the fire, got up and stood above the man. "I brought her up from Nacozari."

He watched the slow wheels turn in Elkhorn's head. Elkhorn had left Loli with Streeter. He said, "Where's Streeter?"

"Dead."

The eyes rolled up, too much white showing. The question pushed up through him. His own question. With the fear in it.

"You're going to kill me here?"

"No."

The body jerked. Hope struck like a blow. Lassiter used it coldly.

"I want the whole story of the Harmony job from you. Everything you know."

Elkhorn, wretched, bedraggled, expanded like a sponge in water. His death sentence was commuted. He could crawl out from under. He laughed. A ragged sound, a gust of relief.

"Sure. Sure. Look, I didn't have any

225

say about it. Not a bit. It was the fat man's game. He put it all together, told me to get you, . . . Let me start over. Frost, the sheriff of Harmony, came to Miguel. His brother had the bank and a wife that Frost wanted. He wanted his brother killed, but done so he could pass it off as part of a robbery. He wanted somebody hung for it so nobody would get curious and start nosing around later.

"Miguel needed a fall guy. You were in town, new. He didn't have any strings on you. With your reputation a jury would love to hang you, they wouldn't look too close at whether you killed the man or not. You were tailor made."

It could be the truth. It had the fat man's mark on it. But there were the first words. The false start. There was something in there with a bad ring to it. Lassiter shook his head slowly.

"I think differently. I think somebody, Blood maybe, got to the fat man

226

with another deal. To get rid of me. Specifically me. I think the rest was window dressing. It took you too much time to get your story straight."

The voice went up, high with strain. "I'll swear it. It's the truth. I know it . . . " Elkhorn faltered again.

Lassiter took out his gun. "How do you know it?"

Elkhorn sweat, licked his lips. He could not find a way to dodge the answer.

"Because Miguel and I talked it over. We talked about seven or eight names before you were mentioned."

"Who mentioned me?"

Elkhorn closed his eyes. "I did."

He waited to be shot. He was not. He opened his eyes and was shocked. Lassiter was smiling. It was the first true smile he had seen on him. He did not understand.

Blood didn't bother Lassiter. He knew him, could handle him. The goad that had sent him chasing Elkhorn down was the possibility that someone he did not recognize as an enemy was working in secret to get him killed. It was a heavy weight that Elkhorn's admission lifted from him.

The day was gone. Lassiter opened his pack, heated food. They ate in silence. Elkhorn's glance touched Lassiter often, speculative, but he did not dare risk asking questions now. He was alive. That was enough for the moment.

Lassiter cared for the horses, tied Elkhorn's hands and feet, knotted the end of the rope around his own wrist. This night he tied the girl too. This night's sleep would be a luxury.

★ ★ ★

"I leveled with you, Lassiter," Elkhorn said. "I told you everything I know. Why don't you let me and Loli go now? I won't get in your way again."

Lassiter looked toward the girl. She huddled in the far curve of the cave, clutched her guitar against her like a doll, watched these men who would decide what disposition to make of her. Sooner or later he would have to decide.

"We'll talk about that when I'm through with you."

"What else do you want with me?" Elkhorn's fear coiled in him again.

"I want that death sentence in Harmony lifted. I'm going to take you over there. You're going to tell the judge what you told me."

Elkhorn groaned.

Lassiter broke the camp. His own horse was trail weary from the long ride out of Mexico. Elkhorn's was fresh. He put Loli into the saddle in front of the man, saw craftiness come in Elkhorn's eyes.

His tone was conversational. "Before you try to make a break I'll tell you. I won't worry about maybe hitting the girl. I'll shoot the horse. You can walk the rest of the way."

Elkhorn did not try. Lassiter did not push. There was no hurry now. He let the animal choose its own gait, rested it often. It still had a way to carry him.

He kept the eastward course, passing below the end of the dry lake. The mountains between hid it from sight. He didn't have to see it to remember it.

Five miles out of Harmony he took them out of the trail, up into the rock breaks, made a camp in a depression. A fire would not be seen from below. After dark he took the girl out of earshot of Elkhorn, stopped where he could keep one eye on the man.

"Loli, after Elkhorn has cleared me, when that sentence is reversed, I'm through with him. What do you want me to do with him?"

Her eyes widened. Nobody had asked her opinion before. She shook her hair back, raised her face. A rising moon touched her.

"Please. Please let me stay with you."

Want of a woman shook him. Hard.

Her softness, her warm youth, her defenselessness pulled at him. The pleading in the light voice would haunt him.

"I can't. I have to ride alone."

Slowly, slowly, she turned toward Elkhorn.

"Don't kill him. He wants me. He keeps other men away."

He touched her elbow, led her back to the fire. Jealousy twisted Elkhorn's face. Lassiter said,

"Time to ride. Get the saddles on."

Elkhorn brought the horses, climbed up, reached for the girl.

"No."

She swung to Lassiter. "You're not going to leave me here?"

"There could be trouble. We'll be back for you."

She turned full around, looking out at the darkness crowded behind the rocks. She put her hand against her mouth.

"If I could have some peyote . . ."

Elkhorn stretched his leg, shoved

his hand into his pocket, brought it out filled with buttons. He reached it toward her. Lassiter intercepted him, pried the fingers open, spilled the pods into his palm.

"One. Just one. You'll have to stay awake, keep up the fire." He gave her the button, put his foot in the stirrup, hesitated, turned back. He took one gun from its holster, shook out the shells, walked back to the blanket, dropped them there. He came back to the horse, handed the gun to the girl. Then he mounted, nodded at Elkhorn, rode out behind the man.

★ ★ ★

The horses' hoofs made only a soft shushing sound in the frothy dust of the street. Harmony was dark except for a light in the sheriff's office. It threw its warm glow out onto the gallows still standing in the plaza. This was manana country. They would take it down on some tomorrow. Elkhorn took them through the dark side of the wide street, out of town, up the north ridge. The judge's house sat on top, overlooking Harmony on one side, overlooking the malevolent lake on the other. Sight of it brought Lassiter's walk across it back to him vividly.

The house was board and batten, unpainted, five rooms. The most pretentious in town. With the moon-light it would not do to tie strange horses at the front rail. Too little out of the ordinary happened in Harmony for it to go unnoticed. They rode to the rear. There was a small barn, the shafts of a buggy tilted up in the open door. There was a single smoke tree in the yard; the dry tufts of wild grass that had been green for a week in early spring were now brown and brittle. Against the house wall the moon picked out the black balls of red geranium blooms on stiff, spindly bushes. The house was dark.

Lassiter got down, drawing his gun,

showing it to Elkhorn as the man dismounted.

"Go ahead of me. Wake him up."

Elkhorn pounded on the door. Inside a dog barked, kept barking. An inner door creaked. A match was struck, a lamp turned up. The judge's voice came through the wall. Lassiter recognized it from the trial.

"Who is it? What do you want?"

Lassiter's lip twitched. "Message about the sheriff. He's in trouble."

A bolt was drawn, the door swung in. Lassiter put his fingers in Elkhorn's belt, the gun muzzle beside his spine, rushed him through. He snaked the door closed with a boot, put Elkhorn between himself and the judge. If he pulled the trigger one slug would do for both of them.

Ellis Vernier was past seventy, a frail figure, his hair white and wispy, his mustache white but still full. He had shrewd eyes, a dignity that kept him standing quiet now. It survived the ludicrous look of the nightshirt.

The gamble now was whether honesty backed up the dignity. Lassiter said,

"Is there anyone else here?"

The eyes were level, steady. They took on scorn.

"No one, Lassiter. You can kill me without interruption."

"I don't intend to. I want that sentence taken off my back."

The scorn increased. "I expect you do. Unfortunately for you, I am too old to be afraid of dying. Intimidation won't help you."

Lassiter stepped back, holstered his gun. "Fair enough. Just sit down at that table and listen to this man. He's known as Elkhorn. He works for Don Miguel. Do you know who he is?"

"Hardly a necessary question." Vernier turned his back, walked to the kitchen table, settled into the facing chair with a regality suited to the bench.

Elkhorn wanted to sit too, his legs were unsteady. Lassiter kept him standing. Elkhorn had trouble beginning. Lassiter tapped a shoulder with his finger.

"We're waiting."

The voice was nervous, shaking with tension, but as he talked the words came stronger, with the urgency of truth.

It was hard to gauge the judge's reaction until the sheriff's name came. He leaned forward then, putting his whole attention on Elkhorn. Most of it had been on Lassiter.

Elkhorn finished, lifted his hands at his sides, dropped them.

"That's the truth. So help me."

Vernier looked away from him. He looked ill. He put an elbow on the table, lowered his forehead to his hand, massaged the bristling white eyebrows. The dog whined from behind a door, scratched at it. A wall clock ticked. The sound grew through the running silence. Vernier said without raising his head,

"There are papers and pens in my study. I'll get them." He walked like a tired man, out of the kitchen.

Elkhorn whispered, hissing, "He'll

get a gun. He'll shoot us both. Draw, damn it."

"You never saw integrity before, did you? He's just had a narrow escape from hanging the wrong man."

Elkhorn didn't believe. The longer the judge was gone the less he believed. Vernier came back without a gun, carrying writing materials. His voice had lost it sureness. He was querulous.

"I couldn't find my specs. Always losing them."

He settled the steel rectangles on his nose, curled the loops over his ears, sat down and wrote his report. He was meticulous, exhaustive, stopping to question Elkhorn, gathering every mite of information he could find. He dried the papers, held them toward Elkhorn.

"You'd better read it."

Lassiter read it across Elkhorn's shoulder. Vernier watched him with possessiveness, as if he had given him life originally. He looked at Elkhorn with less affection, spoke to Lassiter.

He sounded troubled.

"You know, I'd have taken anything either of you said with a lot of salt. Except that a week ago Clay Frost married his brother's widow."

"Would she be a party to murder?"

Vernier was not given to quick judgements. "I . . . don't know. She's strong willed . . . I want you to ride out to the ranch with me. I want to watch her when she sees Elkhorn, when she reads this."

He gave the pen to Elkhorn, ordered him to swear to the confession and sign it, asked that the buggy be harnessed, went for a pair of trousers, pulled a coat on over his nightshirt.

In the yard Elkhorn stopped beside his horse. "I ain't going out there. It's a trick. There'll be a crew. They can take us. With my name on that paper they'll hang me."

Lassiter's gun, in his hand, caught the moonlight. Elkhorn made a strangled sound.

"I did what you wanted. Just give me

a chance to get over the border. I'll take Loli and clear out of this country for good. Frost's the one ought to hang."

"We go to the ranch, give the woman her chance. After that I don't care where you go."

It was ten miles to the ranch. The ride was a letdown, after the weeks of tension. Half a mile of lane led back to the house, a substantial place of logs, two houses really, connected by a Texas gallery. Outhouses, bunkhouse, hay barn, blacksmith shop bulked behind it in a loose square. The corral made a skeleton pattern in the moonlight. It was a prosperous looking spread. Easy enough to see why Frost wanted to marry the widow whether or not he wanted the woman.

Dogs barked as they came into the yard, a light flared in the bunkhouse, a man called from the doorway.

The judge called back. "Ellis Vernier. I want to see Milly."

The door closed, shut the light inside. They rode to the gallery and got down. Elkhorn hung back, suspicion riding him.

"What happens if Frost is here? He's got that whole damned crew against your one gun. You're plain crazy."

16

MILLY FROST was a handsome, black haired woman, tall, carrying herself with pride. The lines of a full bust, of good stalwart hips were evident under the robe that clung against them as she hurried. Through the glass pane in the door they watched her come down the curving stairs, lamp in hand, cross a room of velvet elegance, unlock and pull back the door.

"Ellis." Her voice was throaty, furred with worry. "What's wrong? Is it Clay?"

Lassiter saw the line of white around her mouth, the skin taut over high cheekbones, pinched up under her eyes. The eyes flicked over him, over Elkhorn, went back to Vernier.

Vernier went through the door, talking as he crossed the room, not mentioning the men behind him, not giving her time to prepare herself.

"Milly, bring your light over here. I want you to read these papers."

She did not hesitate. She went after him with a long, quick stride, put the lamp on the crocheted table cover, sat down without flurry, took the papers. There was lean, spare efficiency about her, a control that spurned uncertainty. She read quickly, pulling the sheets down over the thumb that held at the bottom. When she finished she looked up, not at Vernier but at Lassiter, a quick survey, pausing at the hand that rested on the holstered gun, dropping to the boots. She studied Elkhorn. He stood uneasily poised, wanting to bolt. Then she looked at Vernier. Her face was more pinched, paler.

"Ellis, you don't believe this slander?"

The judge put out his lower lip. She did not wait for him.

"You must be losing your mind. These men are wolves, in a corner, grabbing at straws. Clay is ambitious, yes. But he is not stupid. What one

242

shred of proof have you?"

Elkhorn, slow witted, had an answer. In his mind he had shucked the blame from himself onto Don Miguel, onto Clay Frost. It meant freedom from Lassiter. But they had to believe. He was shrill.

"Just how come the sheriff and two deputies happened to be so handy on the back roof of the bank when I went in the front and shot . . . "

The room was abruptly quiet for different reasons. Elkhorn felt the noose jerk tight around his neck. He put up a hand and rubbed it. Vernier and Lassiter watched the woman closely. For the first time she had no ready answer. Those she reached for died borning on her lips. She laid the papers on the table, sat back from them. As far as she could press herself into the chair. The strong voice had a tremble.

"Clay is due here soon. I, at least, want to hear his version."

It was possible she had heard him coming. Hoofs drummed past the porch. Frost's voice called to the bunkhouse.

"Who's here?"

The answer came more faintly. "Judge Vernier and a couple of men."

Inside, the group turned to the door. Lassiter stepped back, away from the others. Frost might panic. The woman misread the move.

"Lassiter. You have a gun. If this nightmare is true, hold your fire."

He did not look toward her. He dropped his hand to his side, watched the door.

Clay Frost had been drinking. He was still pleased over winning the poker game. He shoved the door open without looking through, tramped in, grinned at his wife, said, "Hi, Judge." Then he saw Elkhorn.

He stopped short. He reached for his gun before he saw that Elkhorn wore no belt, before he remembered that he had left his own weapon at the jail. Elkhorn shrank back anyway. Frost slid his eyes to the other man in the room.

After a moment a solidness settled on him. His body pulled tight into itself. The shock on his face passed. Lassiter had not moved. Cunning came to Frost. His mind shut out Lassiter's gun, sloughed off anything that did not fit his instinctive strategy. He spoke to Vernier, hearty.

"So you caught him. Nice. Nice."

Vernier said drily, "Look again. He's the one who's armed."

Milly Frost said, "Clay, did you arrange with Don Miguel that Charles be murdered?"

A rush of blood turned the heavy face scarlet. Frost used it as indignation. "Milly. What the hell are you saying?"

"Did Elkhorn kill him?"

Frost glared at Elkhorn. No one had pointed him out. "I never saw that man before in my life."

Elkhorn snorted. "Oh yes you did. I met you in Tombstone to fix the details. Then we went out to the Clanton ranch together."

The sheriff changed tactics. He

245

looked toward the woman at the table, looked taken aback, puzzled. There was a gun in the table drawer. If he could get to it under the guise of appealing to her for belief, if he could pull if before Lassiter guessed it was there, he had a chance. He spread his hands in front of him, started forward.

"Milly. For God's sake . . . "

The gun exploded. The tip of the barrel rested on the table edge. Lassiter, Elkhorn, Vernier had been watching Frost. They saw him knocked back, saw the hole appear in his shirt chest.

The woman's eyes were set, unmoving on the place where Frost had stood. The gun muzzle leaked smoke. She slid the weapon up as if it were too heavy to lift, slid it onto the table, dropped her hand from it.

Lassiter's gun was leveled on her before the echo of her shot died. He walked backward, put his back against the wall beside the door with the glass. Shouts came from the bunkhouse. Bare feet hit the porch. The door was still open. Men boiled through in red underwear. They stopped, gaped at Frost, on his back on the floor, stared at Elkhorn, dropped at the table base. They looked toward Vernier.

Lassiter said, "Pick up Frost. Take him up to bed." The sheriff was heavy. It would occupy all their hands for long enough. "Judge, you take care of Mrs. Frost. I wouldn't charge her. More likely he killed himself."

He watched the judge bend over the woman, try to draw her to her feet. She sat still as stone. He motioned the gun toward Elkhorn, nodded toward the door. Vernier did not try to stop them. They went out, loosed their horses, left the ranch.

They circled the town, heading back toward the camp in the rocks. Lassiter wanted the gun he had left. It was one of a matched pair, balanced to his hand. He would pick it up and ride north. The girl could have Elkhorn. To leave him alive was the best he could do for her.

The moon was sinking behind the ridge, casting the hillside into deeper blackness. He picked his way among the boulders from memory, unable to see against the light. The fire was a small eye of embers that barely showed him the blanket humped over the small figure. He swung down, walked toward her, bent down to wake her, pulled the blanket away. Then he froze.

There was a handkerchief tied across her mouth. Her hands and feet were roped. His hand went to his gun. There was another hand already on it. Another gun dug into his back.

He would have tried. Twisted away, fought, whipped the blanket at the man to spoil the aim. But if he moved the gun would be trained on the girl. A reflex shot would hit her. He stayed where he was, stayed quiet.

The hand lifted his gun. He did not know who was there. Possibly Vernier had sent a posse on the shorter route through Harmony. Possible the

Chinese had doggedly trailed them.

A voice said, "Okay, Elkhorn. It's us."

It was a voice he had heard in Orillo. One of the fat man's people.

There were five of them. They tied his hands behind his back, gave him to Elkhorn, gave a gun to Elkhorn, cautioned Elkhorn.

"Miguel wants him alive."

Elkhorn stood in front of him, gun whipped him until he fell, taking pleasure. There was pleasure in his questions, laughter in the answering voices.

"How the hell did you happen to turn up?"

"Didn't happen to. Some chinks came tearing down to Orillo and told the fat man you were headed this way. He sent us to cut your trail. We been riding all night."

"But how'd you locate this place?"

"The kid. We heard some shots and came looking and found the fire. There was a coyote yipping. She was

249

scared, shooting at the noise. Where'd you go?"

"Harmony. The bastard made me tell the judge about the Frost job."

Lassiter was on the ground, Elkhorn bent above him, swinging the gun. A voice said.

"Then save your fun. We better clear out of here before he starts a posse after you."

The beating stopped. They hoisted Lassiter onto his horse, tied him there. He was not aware of much of the ride. He roused enough to recognize the littered mouth of Skeleton Canyon when they came down that. His mind was clearing when they crossed the border and camped at the old presidio, but he pretended unconsciousness. They lifted him down, dumped him in the shadow of the old walls.

It was full daylight. They built a fire, ate, sat resting, passing a bottle, joking. They made guesses as to what Miguel would do with him when they reached Orillo. Elkhorn took the girl apart from the others, gave her her guitar, stretched out with his head on her knee, fell asleep, as she played. The others found bits of shade and slept, making up for the lost night.

Lassiter did not sleep. He lay forcing his mind to function, forcing the pain that blurred it into the background. He watched the sun crawl down the western sky, tip the jagged mountains, slip behind them. He watched the girl sleep, leaning against the soft mud wall. She slept restlessly, often half roused by short, convulsive jerkings.

He framed his mouth, sent out a call that seemed to come from a distance, the high, barking cry of a coyote. The girl sat up, her eyes wide. The others slept on, too familiar with the sound even to hear it. He raised his head, beckoned with it.

She looked down at the head in her lap, then back at Lassiter. She lifted a hand, touched her face, as if she were touching his bloody, swollen bruises. She looked toward the other sleeping figures, at the risk. He had little hope that she would take it. Then she did.

Delicately she worked her fingers beneath the head, raised it cautiously, twisted, easing her leg from under it, put it down, supported on the neck of the guitar. She got up and came forward, without words went to work on the knotted rope.

Her nearness, the soft, gentle touch of her fingers, ran through him. Hot. Rank. He cursed himself. Always, the closer danger came the stronger rose the demand of his body. She leaned against him, put her head against his chest, using her teeth to gnaw at the knot they had mockingly tied there. Her warm odor filled his nostrils. He dropped his face into the pale hair, put his lips close to her ear.

"All right. I'll take you with me."

He did not look at what it could mean. But he could not leave her now. They would know that he could not have got free alone. Even if Elkhorn tried to protect her he could not. She would be thrown to Don Miguel. She would pay for this treachery.

The knot came free. She flung the ends apart with a wild swing, in the same movement raised herself and kissed him, covering his bruised mouth with fire.

He lifted her away, got his feet under him, worked them to break up the stiffness. The horses were hobbled in the shade of a cottonwood. He wanted a gun, dared not approach the sleeping men, and put the thought aside. Catfooted he turned the corner of the broken wall, picked up a bridle and saddle as he passed the pile, went toward his own horse. The animal raised its head, tried to move away. He caught it, forced the bit into the mouth, slipped the bridle behind the ears, handed the rein to the girl, stooped for the saddle.

Elkhorn yelled from the far side of the ruin.

Lassiter caught the girl, threw her onto the bare back of the horse, flipped himself up behind her, snatched the rein, yanked it around. He drove his heels hard on the flanks, raced along the shelter of the wall.

They were beyond the wall, in the open. The desert stretched flat for a mile. What growth there was was low, wide spaced, stunted tumbleweed, ground creepers.

Behind them there were shouts. Shots chased them. Bullets drove small geysers of dust up around them. A man stood up from a crouch abreast of them, his trousers around his ankles, dragging at his gun. Lassiter saw him free it, aim it, fire. He pulled the horse's head around. Not in time.

The girl's body heaved up against him, pushed to the side, sagged over his arm. It hung there. He bent over it, kicked the horse, drove on.

The firing died. He was out of range of short guns. A man on a running horse made a hard target for a rifle. He rode a weaving course. The stretching shadows helped. The hills were getting closer. Night was near. Escape was half an hour away. If they did not catch him by then. His tired horse carried a double burden.

He looked back. They were mounted now, riding hard. He looked at the girl, wondered if she were dead. He could drop her if he were sure. He was not.

The land rose. Hummocks gave way to hills, winding swales between. He took the horse in a leap down the sheer bank of a flash flood gully, swung up it, rounded a rocky nose. Patches of purple grew. The horse wanted to slow. He pushed it. He twisted, climbing short draws. He reached a ridge, was exposed to view there, dropped into near dark on the far side. He did not follow the slope to the bottom, instead cut aside, followed a ledge that doubled back, pulled up at a group of boulders.

Across the ridge he heard shouts. They came louder, hoofbeats crossed the crest, then the sounds receded. The men were following the downward draw. He was behind them now. He wanted to be.

He took time to think of the girl. She was still breathing. Shallow. The bullet was lodged somewhere in her. He had no way to reach it.

He could not stay where he was. It would be all right until daylight, then Miguel's men would hunt him down. He was without food, water, gun, saddle. In no condition to push into the mountain wilds.

He shook up the horse. Headed for Orillo.

17

HE rode through the night, camped the day in the foothills above the town. He could look down on the road, see the expanded troop Miguel sent to find him. That could be the only reason for so many riders to leave together. Men did not go in such numbers around here. Mostly they rode alone, inconspicuous, anonymous.

The girl clung to life. He did not know why she wanted it so much. Unless she was too young to understand what must lie ahead for her.

After dark he lifted her to the horse, turned down to the flat, came into Orillo along the alley beside the Casa. The town was uncommonly quiet. Most of its men were away, scouring the country for Lassiter. He turned in behind Debbie's crib, tied the horse, carried the girl to the front door, the only door, kicked it open.

The woman inside sprang up. Her muted, glad cry changed, pushed down to silence when she saw the bloody blouse. She stood without the power to move. He laid the limp figure on the bed, put his ear against the chest. There was no sound. No breath. He did not know when Loli had died. He looked at the woman.

"She's gone, Debbie."

"Who . . . who did it?"

"One of Miguel's crowd. Trying to hit me."

Debbie Dean had no tears. She came to the bed, touched the hand that was still warm, touched the cheek, searched the face.

"Poor little bastard kid. What was it like for her, Lassiter?"

He found a smile. It hurt his beaten face. "In Nacozari I heard her called sunlight that dances on water. She had a guitar. She played well."

A long sigh filled the woman,

258

emptied her, left her shrunken. She looked toward the door.

"I wish you hadn't brought her here."

"Nowhere else I could take her. Should I have left her in the hills for the animals?"

She closed her eyes, tight. "They won't let her be buried in the church here. Not my daughter."

His mouth straightened. "Maybe we can work that out. Let's go see the undertaker. Go tell me when the street's clear."

The undertaker's parlor was behind the hardware store. The same man ran both places. Lassiter pried loose the staple that held the padlock on the rear door, carried the girl's body inside, laid her on the raw boards of the table. He struck a match, saw a closed coffin across a pair of saw horse, went through to the store in front. He found guns, cartridges, loaded a pair, filled his belt, picked up a saddle, took it back to the parlor.

He lifted a corner of the coffin, found it heavy. Debbie was whispering. "Old Jose Santez. Got drunk and drowned in the horse trough. His funeral's tomorrow."

"In the church?"

"Sure."

"Will the coffin be opened?"

"No. He doesn't look very good."

Lassiter pried up the lid, lifted out the rigid body and laid Loli in its place. It was, he thought, a double stroke of luck. Debbie held matches while he nailed the lid tight again. There was a grim satisfaction in her whisper.

"She'll be buried in his grave. I'll like that. But what do we do with him?"

"I've got a use for him, after I pay a call. He'll keep under your bed."

The only question she asked was, "How long?"

"An hour or so."

She helped him carry the clumsy burden, then brought her chair outside and sat before her door. Lassiter walked his horse back to the parlor, saddled it, rode it out of town and tied it. He went to see the fat man.

The mozo did not want to let him in. He put a hand on the man's mouth, picked him up, carried him to the lighted room where he had played chess with Miguel. Miguel was at the table, working out a problem. He was not used to surprises. He watched Lassiter throw the mozo across the floor to the table base, close the door, draw a gun, come toward him. His mouth worked, but the words had no sound.

Lassiter put a boot on the mozo's neck. The man lay prudently still, his face in the tile floor. Lassiter threw a handful of gold coins among the chessmen.

"What I owe you for Elkhorn."

Miguel gaped. He relaxed a little. A very little. The bud lips pursed, the head tipped to one side.

"You killed him?"

"No. I took him to Harmony. He talked to the judge. Your name came up. I expect there'll be a warrant for you. I wouldn't advise you to go to the States again."

The fat lips spread in a relieved smile. "Thank you for the advice. And the money. Where is Elkhorn now?"

"Out with your posse, hunting me."

Miguel toyed with a chess piece. He sounded puzzled and displeased, disturbed by what he did not understand.

"When I gave you permission, helped you find Elkhorn, I expected you to kill him."

"I didn't need to. He signed his own death warrant when he talked to Vernier. He's wanted in the States for murder now. Down here, a man who can tie you to murder wouldn't seem to be in the safest position."

"Such a good mind you have. You look ahead. May I hope that you changed it, came back here to work with me?"

"No. You've got a crowd looking for me outside. I didn't have gun, saddle or water. Orillo was the one place I could come. Will you throw away your ace, let anybody be killed here?"

The Don laughed, loud, happy with the game, raised a finger to command attention.

"But you will not stay forever, Lassiter. When you leave . . . when you leave . . . you won't get far against my wish."

Lassiter put his thumbs in his belt. His grin was a crooked slash in the swollen face.

"A bet on it? What will you put against the buckle?"

The pig eyes brightened. The fat man was enjoying himself, playing his chess with living figures.

"I'll give you odds. Ten thousand gold. And if you won, how would you collect?"

"You can send it to Ho Ling in Weaverville."

Lassiter took his boot off the mozo, left the house. He walked through the plaza, passed the cribs, turned in at Debbie's. She followed him, lighted the lamp while he pulled Jose Santez from under the bed and rolled him on top of it. He gave her instructions as he worked over the corpse, took the belt from his waist, wrapped it, fastened the buckle around the man who had drowned, brought the can of coal oil from the corner, splashed it across the body.

"The horse is in the brush east of town. Give me time to get beyond the alley, then smash that lamp on the bed post. Let the fire catch good, then get out front, yell. Make enough noise to wake up everybody in town. By the time they get here there'll be no stopping the whole row from burning. Wait until the crowd covers you. They won't be watching you. Ease out and run for the horse. I'll see you as far as the railroad, send you wherever you say. You ready?"

Her mouth was parted, her breathing short, rapid. She held the lamp aside, went to stand against him, to lift her mouth. He bent his lips to hers, felt the familiar want.